Harmony's Big Decision

by
Nicola Martin

Published by New Generation Publishing in 2018

Copyright © Nicola Martin 2018

First Edition

The author asserts the moral right under the Copyright, Designs and Patents Act 1988 to be identified as the author of this work.

All Rights reserved. No part of this publication may be reproduced, stored in a retrieval system or transmitted, in any form or by any means without the prior consent of the author, nor be otherwise circulated in any form of binding or cover other than that which it is published and without a similar condition being imposed on the subsequent purchaser.

www.newgeneration-publishing.com

New Generation Publishing

CHAPTER ONE

In an unknown county called Elveshire, located on the eastern boundary of Dorset, there lived a colony of elves. The elves had a king and a queen who lived with their five sons in a big square castle built out of sandy-coloured stone in the town of Elvesbridge at the heart of Elveshire.

Not all the elves lived in or near Elvesbridge. There were many villages and hamlets spread far and wide across the rolling countryside. Along the south coast were two fishing villages where the fisherman lived close to their boats, and brought their catch ashore before being distributed throughout the county by horse and cart. The fishing village of Crocus Poyntz sat to the southwest of Elvesbridge while Ivy Port sat to the southeast of the town.

The majority of Elveshire was made up of pastureland divided up by dry stone walls and thick green hedges. The villages from above looked like little clusters of cottages poking out of a sea of greenery.

Rosemouth, located to the east of Elvesbridge, was one of the smaller villages with whitewashed cottages under thatched roofs. The village made its money mostly by growing and selling flowers, with the odd dressmaker dotted here and there in the village.

Willowsbury was the biggest village of them all to the north of the main town. It was big enough to accommodate what most people would class as a high street running through the middle of it. Along the street sat a butcher's shop, a bakery, a greengrocer, and a florist. If the elves could not get into Elvesbridge then it was where they went for their daily essentials.

To the west of Elvesbridge was a quaint picturesque village called Lilyleigh. Mostly inhabited by farmers and horse dealers, it could be considered the greenest of all the villages. The properties here were mostly stone-built farmhouses with slate roofs.

Surrounding Elveshire were three different rivers that joined together to make a moat around the county. The elves knew the moat most commonly as the boundary line. One of the elves' main rules stated that no one was to cross any of the three bridges that crossed the rivers to the north, the east and the west, because they were forbidden from stepping onto human land.

Among the elves there was one elf that broke the rule on a regular basis. Her name was Harmony Redvers, a young lady who was nineteen years old. It was not because she wanted to break the rule that she crossed the boundary line, it was because she had family and friends in the land of humans.

At the age of two, Harmony was taken by her father to live with the humans after her mother became too ill to look after her. For fifteen years she lived with the humans not knowing she was any different, apart from her ears being different from everyone else's.

Not long after her seventeenth birthday, Harmony returned to the elves at the request of her father. For the first year, Harmony seemed to settle back into the farmhouse that she shared with her father Maurice and her brother Raphael.

It was not until the second year that problems with Harmony began. She had started to distance herself from her father as well as her brother, which confused them both as she had seemed considerably happy during her first year with them. Sensing that his daughter was no longer happy, Maurice decided to bring her a horse home from work.

The horse he brought her was a gorgeous chestnut gelding that Harmony decided to name Tyson. At first it appeared the horse idea would work, until Harmony started disappearing for hours on end with him.

What Maurice did not know was that every time his daughter disappeared she had been breaking the most important rule of the elves by crossing the boundary line, using the west bridge to go and see her human friends.

When Harmony last crossed the boundary line she had nearly been seen by the elves on her return journey across the bridge, so she decided the risk was becoming too great for her to keep seeing her human friends.

CHAPTER TWO

Nearing the end of summer, the weather turned cloudy yet it still felt humid in Lilyleigh. The thick black clouds rolled across the sky deciding where to drop the moisture held within them. As well as carrying rain they threatened to break with claps of thunder.

At the stable-yard, Harmony watched the clouds hoping the rain would hold off as she finished tacking up Tyson. She took off his head-collar before leading him to the middle of the yard so she could mount up, ready to begin her ride.

Harmony rode through the yard before picking up speed once she had cleared the gate, wanting to get under cover of the trees before it started raining allowing her to continue her journey without getting to wet.

As she entered an area of thick woodland, Harmony was startled by a loud clap of thunder overhead, so she took shelter among the trees until the storm had passed.

As they made progress through the woods, Harmony was quickly becoming aware that Tyson was not the bravest horse when it came to thunderstorms. Harmony could feel him tensing underneath her as the claps of thunder cracked overhead, causing a battle for control to begin between horse and rider.

It continued raining when she broke through the other side of the trees, but the thunder had passed over, now nothing more than a faint rumble in the distance which allowed Tyson to relax. As she approached the boundary line she became thankful for the rain, as it meant the other elves had taken cover in the woodland.

Harmony made her way slowly across the stone arch bridge before taking off on the other side, wanting to get out of sight of any elves who might venture out of the trees. She also could not wait to see her boyfriend. They had arranged to meet in a field overlooking Bandit Cove where she used to hang out with all her human friends to have fun.

When Harmony got to the field it surprised her to find that the ground was dry. She dismounted from Tyson before sitting on the grass to wait for her boyfriend to arrive. While she was waiting for him she sat thinking about all the happy memories she had at Bandit Cove with her friends.

Harmony's boyfriend arrived a few minutes later, sitting himself down on the grass next to her. Seeing that she was deep in thought he decided to wait a moment before speaking to her, hoping not to make her jump. "Hi, Harmony, are you okay?" he asked.

"Hello, Damien," said Harmony. "I was just thinking about all the fun times we had together here."

"Is there something bothering you?" Damien asked, knowing her far too well to know there had to be more.

Harmony looked up at him before looking out over Bandit Cove again. "If my father finds out I am here he will kill me," she said nervously.

Damien took hold of his girlfriend's hand. "Don't worry, he won't know you're here," he reassured her.

Harmony continued looking out to sea while playing with the buckle on the end of Tyson's reins, which showed Damien she was not relaxing.

"It's not just your father finding out that you're here is it?" Damien asked.

Harmony shook her head and then looked at the ground pulling her knees towards her before hugging them for comfort.

"Harmony, please, tell me what's wrong?" Damien pleaded.

Harmony looked at Damien and he noticed she had tears rolling down her cheeks.

"I am so sorry, Damien. I am not going to be able to see you anymore," she said, trying to stop her voice from breaking.

Stunned into silence, Damien sat gazing out to sea, trying to process what his girlfriend had just told him.

"Are you okay?" Harmony asked, slightly worried by Damien's silence.

"I just don't get why your real family are trying to keep us apart." Damien replied, explaining the reason behind his silence.

Harmony turned her gaze away from Damien to look at the view once again. "It is complicated," she explained, hoping he would understand.

Damien took hold of Harmony's free hand, causing her to turn her head to look at him.

"I'm your boyfriend, you can tell me anything," he reassured her.

"Breaking up with you is hard enough, so please do not make me explain why," she begged.

"Okay, I'm sorry," he apologised.

Harmony let go of Damien's hand before getting up from the ground.

"Where are you going?" Damien asked.

"I have to get back before they send out a search party to look for me."

Damien stood up to face her. "Can't you stay just a bit longer?"

"I have pushed my luck already; I would rather not push it any further," she replied.

Damien wrapped his arms around Harmony and held her in a warm embrace.

"I am going to miss you so much. Even though we can't be together, I will always love you," he said sadly.

"I am going to miss you, too," she told him, also sounding sad.

Damien let go of her so that she could get back on Tyson. Once she was back on her horse she looked down at Damien one last time.

"Goodbye, Damien," Harmony said finding it hard not to cry.

"Please don't go," Damien begged.

"I have to, it is the only way my family will leave me alone."

"Well then, I guess this is goodbye," he told her.

"I am so sorry, Damien. I wish it could have been different, but this is how it has to be."

Damien walked away with his head hung low. Without looking back at him Harmony gave a kick of her heels, and Tyson cantered towards the boundary line. This moment was painful for her, and as such, she cared little about whether she was seen returning, feeling only a sense of pain for the person she had left behind.

Once Harmony got back across the boundary line she stopped in an empty field so she could be alone to think about her final meeting with Damien. Now that she was alone, Harmony dismounted from Tyson before breaking down in tears. Not only had she said goodbye to her boyfriend, she had said goodbye to her best friend.

CHAPTER THREE

In the village of Lilyleigh, Harmony's father had ridden to the village pond, to find a young elf who could possibly help him make Harmony happy. As he rounded the corner he spotted the young elf he felt could be the one, sat next to the village pond with his horse stood grazing beside him.

The brown horse looked up when it heard Maurice's horse approaching, causing the young elf to look at his horse. "What is it, boy?" the elf asked.

Maurice could not believe how grown-up the young elf looked. It had been a long time since he had seen any members of the royal family because he had removed himself from society and spent most of his time shut away at his cottage.

The elf had medium-length brown hair that looked so silky it almost reflected in the sunlight. His eyes were a light green colour that held a hint of mystery. The young elf looked to be about the same age as Harmony's older brother Raphael, who was in his mid-twenties.

When the elf went back to looking at the pond, Maurice quietly rode closer to him. He stopped his horse as close as he dared go for the time being. Maurice dismounted from the horse and then stood very close to her. He built up a bit of courage before leaving his horse's side to talk to the young elf.

The young elf could see Maurice's reflection in the pond as he approached. "Hello, Goliath," he greeted the elf nervously.

"What can I do for you?" Goliath asked, sounding agitated at being disturbed. He carried on looking at the pond while he waited for a response.

Maurice hesitated before answering. "My daughter Harmony is not happy," he answered.

Goliath did not respond, which caused Maurice to become very tense.

"I was wondering if you would try to cheer her up for me?" he asked.

"I will try to cheer your daughter up for you," Goliath answered calmly.

Maurice relaxed after Goliath agreed to help Harmony. "Thank you, I was completely out of ideas," he said cheerfully.

Goliath got up so that he could face Maurice properly. He looked into Maurice's hazel eyes as he spoke: "There is just one other thing," Goliath added, enjoying being in control of the situation.

"What is it?" Maurice asked. He was worried Goliath was going to change his mind.

"I need her to be able to ride a horse. I enjoy riding therefore I will require her to be able to keep up with me."

Maurice let out a massive sigh of relief. "Harmony has her own horse. She is a brilliant rider. My daughter used to ride with the family a lot until she would no longer talk to us," he informed him.

Okay, I will try to cheer up your daughter. Can you take me to her and I will see what I can do?" Goliath asked.

Maurice got on his horse while Goliath mounted his horse Condor, and then the two of them set off to find Harmony. They stuck to the lands of Elveshire as much as possible, which had become more difficult since the human towns started expanding towards Elveshire. They had expanded so much they were getting close to where the elves lived.

It had turned into a bright sunny day now the storm had passed, hence there were more humans out and about. Luckily the humans were too busy to notice a couple of elves ride by.

"How come you are mixing with the humans?" Goliath asked.

"We have no choice. The human towns are always expanding, causing them to push into our territory. We try our best not to be seen, but even that is not easy anymore," Maurice answered.

As the two of them were riding along they caught a glimpse of Harmony sat with her horse straight in front of them.

Once Harmony spotted her father she got up from the ground before turning around and walking away. Once she had got far enough away, Harmony stopped so that she could mount on to Tyson. Harmony turned him to face her father and his friend before charging her horse past them, causing Maurice's horse Bluebell to back into Condor.

Goliath turned to Maurice. "Is she always like that?" he asked.

"No, she only started acting like that recently," Maurice answered. He sounded annoyed with his daughter.

Goliath turned Condor so he could go after Harmony. Goliath was cantering along when he realised that Harmony started getting too close to the boundary line. "HARMONY, STOP!" he shouted.

Harmony ignored him and just carried on heading for the boundary line.

Goliath shouted again, this time with more urgency in his voice. "Harmony, please stop!" he begged.

"WHY SHOULD I?" Harmony asked, shouting back.

"We are getting too close to the boundary line."

Harmony stopped Tyson before turning to face Goliath. When he caught up with her, Goliath stopped his horse next to her.

"How come you care so much?" Harmony asked, slightly out of breath.

Goliath was about to answer when Harmony decided she had not finished.

"No one ever talks to me, especially since I have returned from the humans. Now you are worried about me getting too close to them," she added resentfully.

"Look, we are elves, they are humans. Your father has been trying to teach you that for the past couple of years. We do not mix with them," Goliath told her, also sounding slightly angry trying to make her understand the elves' rule about the humans. He did not shout, hoping Harmony would not run away again.

"Anyway, what is your name?" Harmony asked, deciding to change the subject before getting another lecture.

"Sorry, Harmony, my name is Goliath," he replied, looking at Harmony with inspecting eyes.

Goliath noticed that Harmony shared the same hazel-coloured eyes as her father, although her eyes did not sparkle with happiness as he had expected from a beautiful young lady. Her dark blonde hair hung down to her shoulders. For Goliath it was strange to see a girl with such short hair, as the female elves allowed their hair to grow down their backs.

Harmony and Goliath started to take a slow ride back to Harmony's cottage. On the way they bumped into Harmony's brother, Raphael, who decided he would ride alongside them on a lovely liver chestnut mare.

Goliath looked at the two siblings, noticing the similarities between them as well as their differences. Their hair appeared to be the same colour, reaching down to roughly the same length. While Harmony had her father's hazel eyes, Raphael shared his mother's blue eyes.

Harmony was suspicious as to why her brother would suddenly turn up seemingly out of nowhere. "What are you doing here, Raphael... spying on me?" she asked curiously.

"No. Father sent me to tell you it was time for you to return home," he answered defensively.

Harmony looked at Goliath.

"Father also told me to tell you that Goliath is welcome to come and stay for as long as he likes," Raphael added.

The three of them carried on riding back to the cottage where Harmony lived with her family. As they were riding along in silence, the only noises to be heard were the birds singing as well as the horses hooves on the solid track.

Not enjoying the silence, Harmony decided to break it by quizzing Goliath. "So, Goliath, whereabouts do you live?" she asked curiously.

Raphael listened intently.

"Oh. Well... I just travel around really," Goliath answered hesitantly.

Raphael looked ahead, suddenly alarmed. "Hold on," he instructed.

Harmony and Goliath stopped when he did. The two of them looked at Raphael, confused as to why he wanted them to stop.

"We had better hide or take a detour as there is a group of humans heading straight towards us," Raphael informed them.

As Raphael turned his horse, Goliath followed starting to head in the opposite direction to where they had been heading. It did not take any of them long to realise there was a big problem. Tyson had decided that he did not want to turn around to follow Raphael and Goliath.

Harmony looked round at the boys. "What are we going to do? Tyson and I are not exactly going anywhere," she said, annoyed that her horse had picked that moment not to cooperate with her.

Goliath looked at Raphael hoping he would have a solution to their current problem. When it looked like Raphael was not going to suggest a solution, Goliath had an idea. "I think Harmony should get on Condor, then you two should get out of here. I will try leading Tyson to catch you two up."

Harmony dismounted from Tyson so she could give him to Goliath who had dismounted from Condor. She walked over to Condor who was taller than Tyson, which meant Goliath had to give her a leg up onto his back. The stirrups on Condor's saddle were too long, and for that reason, Harmony crossed them over the saddle in front of her. It was lucky for Harmony that she was a good enough rider that she did not require them.

Once Harmony was on Condor she went with her brother to get away from the humans. When Tyson started going in the right direction, Goliath stopped him so that he could quickly get on to catch up with Harmony and Raphael.

When Harmony and Raphael were a safe distance away from the humans, they stopped to wait for Goliath. As soon as he got to them, Goliath dismounted before going to help Harmony down from Condor.

Harmony got down from the horse, which was further from the ground than what she was used to. When Harmony's feet hit the floor, Goliath put his hands on her waist to make sure she did not stumble backwards.

Harmony looked up at him. "Thank you," she said gratefully.

Goliath looked down at Harmony. "You are welcome."

Harmony and Goliath looked into each other's eyes for a moment before she walked over to her brother to get Tyson. Harmony and Goliath settled back on their own horses before they carried on the journey home, which they eventually completed without any more obstacles.

CHAPTER FOUR

When Harmony, Raphael and Goliath arrived at the stableyard the three of them dismounted from their horses. Once they were all on the ground Harmony turned to look at Goliath and Raphael.

"Could you two take Tyson's tack off and then put him in his stable please?" she asked politely.

"Of course, we can untack Tyson for you," Goliath replied as he took Tyson's reins from Harmony.

Harmony started to walk away from the stables towards the garden gate.

"Where are you going?" Raphael asked suspiciously.

Harmony turned to look at her brother. "I am going to see Father," she replied, sounding agitated that her brother was being nosey.

Harmony turned away from Raphael to continue walking to the cottage through the back garden. When she reached the backdoor she made her way into the kitchen. As she looked up she noticed her father stood looking at her from the entrance hall.

Maurice had not expected to see his daughter in the kitchen. He was even more surprised when she walked towards him.

"Hello, Father," Harmony greeted him. She opened her arms to give her father a hug.

Maurice could see what his daughter was going to do so he backed away from her. When he started backing away, Harmony stopped. Maurice could see the hurt in his daughter's eyes that he had backed away from her hug. "What are you doing here?" he asked accusingly.

Harmony looked at her father, confused by his question. "Raphael told me that you had sent him to tell me it was time I came home," she answered defensively. She watched her father's expression knowing that would tell her if he had wanted her home.

"I never sent your brother to get you," Maurice informed her.

It sounded to Harmony like her father was accusing her of making the story up. Harmony did not like her father's tone because she knew what was coming next, hence she said it before her father could. "Let me guess. I am sleeping in the horsebox again," she said sarcastically. Not wanting to be near her father any longer Harmony left the cottage to sit in the garden.

Harmony walked straight past her brother, heading for the bench. She picked up the book she had placed under it that morning, wanting to do something relaxing. When she opened her book, she hoped her brother would leave her in peace.

On the grass Raphael picked up a blade of grass placing it between his thumbs. He blew on the grass which made a whistling sound that caused Harmony to look up from her book. Raphael blew on the grass again, causing her to laugh as she remembered whistling with grass as a child. After they had spent a few minutes reminding Harmony of her childhood, the two of them returned to the cottage.

Raphael entered the cottage followed by a nervous Harmony, who hoped her father would now be in the living room. When she got into the boot room she quickly glanced into the kitchen. Harmony could see that her father was not in the kitchen therefore she took her boots off. Harmony walked into the kitchen to find her two cousins sat at the dining table.

The young man had medium-length blond hair and was sat slouched in one of the chairs at the kitchen table. His blue eyes were focused on Harmony. Across the table from him sat a young lady. She had the same bright blonde hair and piercing blue eyes as her brother. Unlike her brother, the young lady sat perfectly straight in her chair watching Harmony.

"What are you up to, cousin?" the young man asked suspiciously.

"Not much, Amos, just trying to avoid Father as usual," Harmony answered innocently.

Amos looked at his sister, not completely convinced.

"May I ask, why are you trying to avoid Uncle Maurice?" the young lady asked.

Harmony sat in the spare chair next to Amos, causing him to straighten up. Her cousins were paying even more attention now, hoping the answer was going to be a good one.

"No reason," Harmony answered nervously.

Harmony's cousins misread the reason for her nerves. They were under the impression she was worried her father might overhear their conversation. What Harmony's cousins did not realise was that they were making her feel uncomfortable because it seemed like they were interrogating her.

"If you are worried about your father overhearing he will not because he went out for a while," Amos told her.

The young lady was looking at Harmony like she was trying to get a deep dark secret out of her.

"Honestly, Rhoda. There is no reason as to why I am trying to avoid my father." Harmony was becoming agitated.

Harmony slid her chair away from the table before getting up to leave the uncomfortable atmosphere of the kitchen, which had been caused by her cousins. She walked into the entrance hall wanting to take advantage of her father's absence. She walked straight up the stairs to her bedroom.

When Harmony was safely inside her bedroom she put some music on by her favourite human band before grabbing a holdall from under her bed. Harmony quickly went around her room grabbing anything she might want in the horsebox. Knowing she would not be going back to the cottage when her father returned home, she double checked that she had everything. Once Harmony had packed everything she turned her music off before quickly going back downstairs.

Not knowing how long she had, Harmony did not want to make any unnecessary stops in the cottage. She felt pleased when she found the kitchen deserted, not wanting to experience another interrogation by her cousins, which would certainly have delayed her exit from the cottage. Harmony did not relax until after she had left the cottage behind her.

CHAPTER FIVE

Harmony put her bag in the horsebox and then made her way over to the stable-yard to put the rest of the horses to bed. Harmony spent longer with one horse than she did all the other horses. The horse was a beautiful grey, out of all the horses in the stables it appeared to be the oldest.

Harmony returned the horsebox to make herself some dinner in the small kitchen. She would never admit it, but she preferred sleeping in the horsebox as it meant being closer to the horses.

When Maurice returned home he entered through the front door. As he felt tired he went straight up to bed, never sparing a thought for the kind of night his daughter would be having.

The next morning Harmony got up early to see to the horses. After getting dressed she went to the stable-yard. First Harmony greeted Tyson before moving to the stable next door to greet the grey horse.

The first job of the morning was turning all the horses out in the field. To get the job done quicker, she turned the horses out two at a time. Now all the stables were empty it was time to do the mucking out.

The boys always complained if they had to do the mucking out, but Harmony always reminded herself that it was all part of the job of owning horses. It always seemed worse though after all the horses had been kept in as there were more stables to do.

Harmony worked in silence listening to the horses enjoying themselves in the field. Thinking that she was alone, it startled her when someone touched her on the shoulder.

"Sorry," the person apologised after he made her jump.

Harmony turned around to find Amos stood behind her. She sighed before getting back to work hoping he had not come to interrogate her again. Amos walked into the stable to lean against the wall.

"What do you want, Amos?" Harmony asked annoyed.

"I came to see how you were. You seemed a little preoccupied yesterday," Amos replied innocently.

Harmony walked over to the wheelbarrow to move it out of the stable. Amos followed her even though it appeared the small talk was over. As they approached the next stable, the two of them noticed Goliath heading their way.

Goliath stopped next to Harmony. "Amos, could you give me a minute alone with your cousin please?" he asked.

"Of course, Prince Goliath," Amos answered as he bowed to the prince.

Harmony looked at Amos, playing the words in her head making sure she heard him correctly. "What did you just call him?" she asked bewildered.

The two boys looked at Harmony to see if she was being serious.

"He called me, Prince Goliath."

"You did not know that he was a prince?" Amos asked, chuckling to himself.

"No, I did not know. I have been living with humans for the past fifteen years in case you had forgotten."

Amos walked away leaving Goliath alone with Harmony as he had asked.

"Well then. When were you planning on telling me that you are a prince?" Harmony asked.

Goliath hesitated. "I am not going to lie to you," he told her.

Harmony rolled her eyes. "That will be a first," she said sarcastically.

Goliath waited to see if she would listen. When he felt sure she would not interrupt, he began to answer Harmony's question. "I had hoped that I would not need to tell you who I truly am," he answered softly. He reached forward to take hold of Harmony's hands.

Harmony pulled away from him causing Goliath to drop his hands to his sides.

"You had better go muck out Condor's stable while I take Tyson to the sand school. I have got a competition coming up, so I need to fit in as much practice as I can," Harmony told him sternly.

Goliath took the shavings fork from Harmony allowing her to go to the field. He watched her walk to the field to get Tyson, before walking to Condor's stable to muck it out knowing Harmony would check to make sure it had been done.

When Harmony got back to the yard with her horse she was pleased to see Goliath had gone. She spent a lot of time grooming Tyson before tacking him to go jumping. Once Tyson had been tacked up, she mounted up and rode him round to the paddock.

When Harmony got around to the sand school, she had to reach down to open the gate. Knowing that Goliath could probably see her, she hoped Tyson would cooperate. He cooperated with her to open the gate, however, it was when she needed to close the gate that Tyson decided he had had enough of being cooperative. Not wanting Goliath to come over to help her, she decided to push the gate closed hoping it would latch itself. Harmony felt relieved when she heard the latch catch.

Now that she was securely in the sand school, Harmony started working Tyson. She started off by riding him at different paces to warm him up before moving on to the jumping work. As Harmony was riding around the paddock she could tell Tyson could sense something in the trees. She started listening carefully for any movement. When everything seemed still and quiet she turned her attention back to working him.

After finishing the mucking out, Goliath decided to hide in the trees to watch Harmony working her horse. He was stood watching her jump when he realised how much he liked her. Goliath sighed, looking at the ground before looking up at Harmony again. "I love you, Harmony," he whispered to himself.

What Goliath had not realised was that he was not the only person watching Harmony in the school. Across the other side of the sand school, also hidden in the trees, was Harmony's human boyfriend Damien.

Damien stayed hidden in the thickest part of the trees hoping not to be seen. He also stood thinking about how much he still loved Harmony and that he could never let her go. "I love you more than you will ever know, and I will never give up on us being together," he whispered to himself.

Damien turned away, knowing he should leave before anyone saw him. It was hard for him to leave Harmony behind, but he knew for now it was what was best for her. He looked back at her one more time before exiting the trees.

Harmony was now walking Tyson around the sand school to cool him down after his workout. Goliath knew that he needed to get back to the yard before she realised he had been watching her. When Goliath got back to the yard, Maurice was stood waiting for Harmony to return.

"Where is my daughter?" Maurice asked.

Goliath looked towards the sand school. "She is jumping Tyson in the sand school," he said.

Maurice seemed to accept Goliath's answer. "Can you tell her that her tea is ready," he said.

"I will do it now," Goliath replied.

Maurice turned away from Goliath and made his way back to the cottage, while Goliath made his way over to the sand school to deliver Maurice's message.

As soon as Harmony spotted him she rode over to the school fence. "What do you want?" she asked.

"Your father asked me to tell you that your tea is ready," Goliath replied.

"I will have it after I have sorted Tyson out," she told him sharply.

Goliath walked away, not wanting to get angry with the young lady he loved.

Harmony rode Tyson back to the yard to untack him. While she was taking care of him she began to cry. Tyson turned his head to nudge her reassuringly, so she gave him a hug. "Oh, Tyson, I miss Damien so much. I hate these stupid elf rules that are keeping us apart," she told him.

Tyson turned his head, giving her a comforting hug. Harmony pulled away wiping the tears from her eyes. Once she had pulled herself together she untied her horse to put him in his stable, and then stroked him one last time before returning to the cottage.

Inside the kitchen Goliath and Raphael were just sitting down to eat their tea. On the kitchen table Harmony spotted her plate placed upon it, she walked over taking a seat next to her brother.

Goliath kept watching Harmony, waiting for her to make conversation with her brother. When she never spoke, he knew there had to be more to her unhappiness than met the eye. Goliath also sat waiting for Raphael to say something to Harmony. When Raphael remained silent it occurred to him that he was used to her silence, so he knew better than to get her to talk.

Harmony finished eating her meal and then took her plate over to the sink. She put her plate on the side before heading towards the backdoor.

"Where are you off to?" Raphael asked curiously.

Harmony turned to look at her brother. "I am going back to the horsebox," she answered. She did not wait for a response, instead she just walked out of the cottage.

That night Harmony lay awake, thinking about the way her father treated her. While she was silently thinking, she could hear a horse whinnying from the stables. Knowing that it was Tyson it comforted her enough for her to fall asleep.

For the rest of the week Harmony's days were divided between looking after the horses, working Tyson in the jumping paddock and avoiding being alone with Goliath. To help with avoiding Goliath she continued to keep him busy at the stables, it kept him away from her as well as giving her more time to exercise Tyson. Harmony also enjoyed the amusement of watching a prince doing manual labour.

CHAPTER SIX

It was nearing the end of the first week with Goliath when Harmony had run out of excuses to keep him away from her. She was stood grooming Tyson when he approached.

"How come you have been doing so much jumping over the past week?" Goliath asked.

"I have a competition tomorrow, meaning I needed to practise as much as possible."

Goliath could not believe his ears. "Are you crazy?" he said angrily. "Does your father, brother or cousin know what you are up to?"

"No, they do not know about it."

Goliath looked nervous. He did not like the quick response she had given him.

Harmony looked at the ground before looking back up to Goliath. "Can you keep a secret?" she asked nervously.

"Of course I can," he answered reassuringly.

Harmony stood silently, as she could not decide if she should tell Goliath the reason she had not told her family about the horse show. After giving it much thought she came to a decision.

Goliath stood waiting, wondering what Harmony was going to tell him. By the amount of time it was taking her to tell him, he knew it could not be anything good. It hurt him that Harmony did not trust him enough to tell him the reason, no matter how bad it was.

"I have sent a text message to the very large human family I used to live with inviting them to the competition. I would also like it if you would come to support me," she told him.

Goliath was unsure about going to an event among humans on their territory. The one thing that convinced him was that it would mean some time alone with Harmony. "Of course, I will come with you to the competition. I just have one condition though."

"What is the one condition?" Harmony asked. She was ready to object to the condition straight away, even though she had not considered that it might be something he would be doing.

"I will be staying hidden in the shadows of the trees. While I think of it, I would appreciate it if you would keep your ears hidden," Goliath replied.

Harmony smiled. That condition she would be able to cope with. While Harmony had been talking to Goliath she had tacked up Tyson.

"Are you going jumping again?" Goliath asked.

"Not today. Tyson enjoys a good hack the day before a competition, so I always take him out for a couple of hours." Harmony untied Tyson before leading him to the middle of the yard to mount up. Once she was on horseback she checked the girth and her stirrups before setting off on her hack.

After watching Harmony set off on her ride, Goliath went to the equipment shed to get a broom. He decided to impress Harmony by having the yard swept by the time she got back. While he was sweeping, Maurice turned up at the yard, looking to see if Harmony was there. Goliath stopped sweeping so that he could talk to him.

Maurice turned as he heard Goliath approaching.

"Can I ask you something?" Goliath asked.

"Of course," Maurice replied.

"Is it okay with you if I take your daughter out for the day tomorrow?" Goliath asked nervously.

"It is fine with me as long as you stay away from humans," Maurice replied sternly. He walked away back to the cottage to let Goliath get on with the stable chores.

After finishing the chores, Goliath went to the gate of the sand school to wait for Harmony. As he saw her approaching he got ready to walk alongside her back to the yard.

As Harmony came over the brow of the lane she could not believe her eyes when she spotted Goliath stood next to the sand school gate waiting for her. He had been so nice and helpful to her that she started to become suspicious of what he was up to.

"How was your hack?" Goliath asked as he walked along beside her.

"It felt fine. I think he is definitely ready for tomorrow," she replied enthusiastically.

When they reached the yard, Harmony dismounted from Tyson.

"What are you going to do now?" Goliath asked.

Harmony tied Tyson up outside his stable. "Now the hard work begins," she replied, handing him Tyson's saddle.

Goliath waited to be given the horse's tack before going to the tack room, wanting to be near Harmony.

Harmony followed him to the tack room to get what she needed to wash Tyson. Once she had everything she needed she made her way out of the tack room with Goliath following her.

"Do you need a hand?" Goliath asked.

"Yes please, that would be really helpful," she said, and then untied Tyson before leading him over to the yard tap which had a hosepipe connected to it.

At the yard tap Goliath took hold of Tyson's lead rope allowing Harmony to run the hosepipe over the horse to make him wet. He watched her as she rubbed the shampoo into Tyson's coat, concentrating hard to make sure she did not miss any bits. He held Tyson in place while she thoroughly rinsed off all the bubbles.

When Tyson was clean, Harmony took his lead rope from Goliath before the two of them walked him back over to his stable to tie him up outside.

"Have you got a lot to do?" Goliath asked.

Harmony sighed. "More than I dare to think about," she replied.

After cleaning Tyson, they put him in his stable for the night. Harmony took the equipment she had used to wash him back to the tack room. While she was there, she collected the soap and cloth for cleaning the tack, taking it to the horsebox. To make getting ready in the morning easier she had decided to sleep in the horsebox after she had completed all her preparations.

Goliath decided to head back to the cottage, leaving Harmony to finish off her preparations without any distractions or interruptions.

After Harmony had finished her show preparations she made herself some tea in the small kitchen, before going to bed ready for her early start the next morning.

CHAPTER SEVEN

The next morning Harmony had got up before dawn. She started loading everything she would need in the horsebox while waiting for Goliath to come out of the cottage.

In the cottage, Goliath was trying to get ready as quietly as possible hoping not to wake anyone up. When he got downstairs he was surprised to find Harmony's family were already sat at the kitchen table. "What are you all doing up?" he asked.

"We decided to go with you and Harmony on your day out," Maurice said.

Goliath felt nervous as he knew Harmony's family would not approve of the location for their day out. "Okay, are you ready to go?" he asked, knowing that Harmony would want to get going.

The boys finished their breakfast and then made their way to the stable-yard. On the way to the stable-yard Goliath informed the others that they would need to get their horses ready for travelling.

While the boys got their horses ready for travelling, Goliath informed Harmony about her family joining them for their day out. This was met with an anxious look from Harmony, who was concerned with how her father would react around humans.

Once all the horses were ready for travelling, Harmony began loading them into the horsebox. She loaded the boys' horses first before loading Tyson as he would be the first horse to need unloading when they reached the show ground.

Goliath was stood watching Harmony load the horses when Raphael approached him.

"Did Harmony seem okay with us joining you on your day out?" Raphael asked.

"She seemed happy enough about it," Goliath answered.

While the last of the horses were being loaded, the boys climbed into the horsebox, all except Raphael. He waited so that he could help his sister lift the ramp on the horsebox. After the ramp had been secured Harmony climbed into the horsebox followed by her brother.

Once everyone had climbed in, Goliath began the journey to the show ground. On the way Harmony decided she had better give everyone a warning as to where they were going to be spending the day.

"I have a confession to make," Harmony said nervously.

"A confession to what?" Maurice asked.

Harmony hesitated, knowing her father could explode with anger at any moment. "We are going to a horse show which I am going to be competing in. I should also warn you that there will be humans there," she answered, feeling relieved that she had told them the truth.

Raphael decided to speak before his father could say something he might regret. "We will be hiding in the trees to keep out of sight of the humans," he informed her.

This was no surprise to Harmony as Goliath had already decided that that was what he was going to do. "That is fine with me, Goliath is doing the same thing," she told them.

For the rest of the journey, the boys were asking Harmony questions about the competition. She explained to them about the event as well as the class she was competing in at the show. The only person who did not show any interest in the competition was Maurice, which surprised no one.

It was not long before they arrived at the show ground, which already looked quite busy. Goliath parked the horsebox in a space by the trees and they all got out, uncertain as to what they were going to do while they waited for Harmony to get ready.

"I am just going to get my entry number," Harmony informed them as she walked off.

As Harmony walked away, Maurice whistled to get his daughter's attention. When she looked round her father pointed at his ears. Knowing what he meant she quickly pulled her hair over her ears before carrying on.

Goliath unloaded Tyson from the horsebox; before securing him ready for Harmony to groom when she returned. As he tied the horse to the horsebox he worried about what Maurice thought of him as he had broken the one rule Maurice had made for Goliath and Harmony's day out.

Harmony returned to the horsebox with her number so that she could get her horse as well as herself ready for the jumping class she was competing in. "I am in the third from last pairing," she informed them.

"Why are you in pairs?" Goliath asked.

"We race against each other over an identical course of jumps set up parallel to each other. The winner of each race will move on to the next round," she said.

The boys smiled at her now that they understood what was going to happen in the competition. Raphael tapped his father on the shoulder as he looked towards the stands. Maurice turned to look at his son to see what he wanted.

"Father, we had better go and hide in the trees as the competition will be starting soon."

Maurice made his way toward the trees followed by Raphael and Amos. Goliath watched them leave wishing he was going with them, but he could not because he stayed behind to help Harmony.

As Harmony was rushing to finish getting Tyson ready, she glanced up to where the general public were entering the stands. As she looked closer she noticed every member of the human family she had lived with enter the stands.

Goliath looked up to notice Harmony had frozen in place, concerned he walked over to her to find out what was wrong. "Are you okay?" he asked, following her gaze to the entrance of the stands.

"No, I am not okay. I have just seen every member of the human family enter the stands."

Now that everything was ready, Goliath decided to make his getaway. "I am going to go and find your family. You had better get on Tyson as you two are up next," he informed her.

"See you later," Harmony said nervously.

"See you later, and good luck," Goliath told her, and then walked off to join her family.

Harmony walked over to Tyson to take his head collar off. She took hold of his reins leading him away from the horsebox. When she was far enough away she stopped to tighten Tyson's girth before getting on ready to head to the warm-up area. Before leaving, she sat for a moment trying to calm her nerves. Once she felt settled, Harmony rode off ready to compete.

In the warm-up area the crowd could be heard cheering and clapping for the competitors who were in the arena. Harmony tried to block the crowd out of her mind as she started warming Tyson up. As her turn got closer, Harmony found it harder to keep herself calm. She had not been warming up for long when her number was called out. She made her way over to the entrance of the arena, where a lady with a clipboard stood waiting to tell the competitors which course of jumps they would be jumping.

The lady looked up at the two girls. "Harmony, you will be jumping the course on the left. Lucy, you will jump the course on the right-hand side of the arena."

Lucy walked into the arena first heading down the right-hand side; Harmony followed her before heading down the left-hand side. As she rode to the start, Harmony was trying to block the noise of the crowd from her mind.

At the bottom of the arena, the girls turned at exactly the same time to start jumping the course of fences. Lucy was just ahead as they jumped the first few jumps. As she turned for the fourth jump, Lucy misjudged the angle, turning too tight causing the horse to knock the jump down.

Harmony knew that she had to jump clear as well as stay close to Lucy if she wanted to win. As they jumped the final jump Lucy was still in front. Harmony pushed Tyson as hard as she could hoping he would pick up speed. When they crossed the finishing line Tyson had just managed to get his nose in front. Harmony slowed him to a walk before patting him on his neck.

The crowd were clapping and cheering for them. Harmony looked up to the stands to see the human family clapping for her. She then turned to look at the elves stood in the trees to see that they were also clapping for her. She watched them turn to leave the trees to go back to the horsebox. Just as Amos turned to leave, he fell over something. As Harmony rode out of the arena she was trying her hardest not to laugh at her cousin.

CHAPTER EIGHT

After leaving the arena, Harmony returned to the horsebox where the boys were stood waiting for her. When she saw them, they were still laughing at Amos, so she finally gave in and started laughing with them.

At the horsebox Harmony dismounted from Tyson then put his head collar on, which was still tied to the horsebox. They were all starting to gain their composure from laughing when they heard a voice call Cara. Harmony looked up, recognising the voice that called her name.

"What did they just call you?" Goliath asked sounding defensive.

"The humans called me Cara when I lived with them," Harmony answered.

The humans that Harmony had invited to the competition approached the elves stood by the horsebox.

"Hello, Cara," her human mother greeted her.

Harmony smiled at them hoping no one would notice how nervous she was about the current situation. "Let me introduce you to my birth family. From left to right we have my father Maurice, my older brother Raphael, my cousin Amos, and on the end is Goliath, a family friend," she informed the humans.

While each of them exchanged greetings, Maurice was reluctant at first to acknowledge them. Harmony seemed pleased that her birth family were being civilised with the humans.

"Now that I am back with my birth family, I am called Harmony. I would like it if you would call me by my elf name," Harmony informed them.

"What did you say?" one of the humans asked.

"I am an elf, I would like you to call me by my elf name," Harmony answered a little louder than she had intended to.

Everyone who heard turned to look at her. Harmony slowly pulled her hair back behind her ears revealing her pointy ears. Maurice could not believe his eyes at what his daughter was doing. He walked away looking disappointed at what his daughter had done. Harmony looked at her brother who also gave her a disapproving look before going after his father.

Raphael caught up to his father near the trees they had hidden in. "Father, are you okay?" he asked.

Maurice turned to face his son. "I cannot believe your sister just did that. I mean, after all the things we told her about the rules," he said angrily.

Raphael looked down at the ground. "I know what you mean but Harmony has always been a rebel. She is also different from us. She has seen the life of humans in a way that we have not," Raphael explained, hoping he could bring his father around.

Neither Maurice nor Raphael knew that Harmony was stood behind them listening to their conversation.

"So that is what you really think of me," Harmony said, the hurt clear in her voice.

Raphael turned to find his sister stood behind him. "You do not think about things, you just do them!" he exclaimed.

"Well that is where you are wrong," she told them calmly.

"What do you mean?" Raphael asked. He was now confused by his sister's words.

"I had actually planned to tell the humans that I am an elf weeks ago. I knew exactly what I was doing. I also knew how I wanted to do it," she said.

"You planned this. You, had planned, this. You had planned to upset your own father!"

Harmony looked at her brother surprised he was taking their father's side. "Yes, I had planned it. Father had hurt me so many times I wanted him to know what it felt like."

"I understand that, but do you not think with the humans moving closer we have enough to worry about. There is also the fact that your mother is dead, which your family have been keeping from you," Goliath told Harmony from his position behind her.

"No, she can't be, she just went away for work," Harmony told him.

"That is just the story they told you so you would not leave again. They thought that as long as you wanted to see your mother you would stay with the elves," Goliath informed her.

"Is that true?" Harmony asked looking at her brother.

Raphael looked away unable to look at his sister.

"IS IT?" Harmony asked, shouting because no one had answered.

"Yes, it is true," Maurice answered confidently.

Raphael finally managed to look at his sister. "Harmony, are you okay?"

Everyone could see that Harmony's face had turned pale, and they were concerned that she was going to pass out at any moment.

"I am fine," she said, trying to keep her voice steady. She looked up at her brother wanting answers. "When did this happen?"

"Not long after you had gone to live with the humans," Raphael said.

They were both finding it hard to keep their voices steady, then Raphael noticed his sister crying.

"How did she die?" Harmony asked, sounding very upset.

"I do not know the answer to that," Raphael answered truthfully.

Harmony looked at the ground. "I would like to be on my own," she informed them quietly trying to hide the tears that were streaming down her cheeks.

As none of the boys were leaving her alone, Harmony walked past them to find a quiet spot away from them.

"Are you okay?" Goliath asked as Harmony walked past him. He was now regretting telling her about her mother.

Harmony never answered him, she just carried on walking away from the boys. As she was walking along Harmony came to a patch of grass surrounded by trees. She sat down on the grass to think about her mother. Now that her mother was gone, she felt as lonely as ever. Harmony's mother had been the only one to worry about her being with the humans. She sat waiting for the tears to come as it sank in that she was never going to see her mother again.

Back at the horsebox, Tyson had decided he wanted to be with Harmony. He was doing everything possible to break the rope tying him up. Goliath tried to calm him down, but he was fighting a losing battle.

Tyson finally managed to break the rope before backing away from the horsebox then racing off to find Harmony. When Tyson got to her he held his head low and turned it to face away from her. It was as if he knew what he had done was wrong.

"It is okay, Tyson. I am glad you broke away from the horsebox, just do not go making a habit of it," Harmony told him. She seemed slightly happier to see her horse.

Tyson moved to stand next to Harmony and then lowered his head so that she could stroke him. While Harmony was stroking him she spotted her human boyfriend Damien across the clearing from them. Harmony got up from the ground to move nearer to him. She ended up stopping a few feet away.

"Damien, what are you doing here?" she asked.

"The family you lived with told me about the show so I decided to come and see my girlfriend," Damien said.

Harmony moved closer to Damien. "I am sorry you had to find out about me being an elf like that. I hope you still like me?" she asked nervously.

Damien took a step towards Harmony. "Of course I still like you. I just called you my girlfriend didn't I. Besides, I always knew you were different from us, I just didn't know what it was. It was also very brave of you to let everyone know that you are an elf," he said reassuringly.

Harmony could hear someone approaching them.

"You have to go; if my family catches us I will never get to see you again," she told him.

"How will I know when I can see you again?" Damien asked.

Harmony looked round to see how much time they had. "I will send you a text message."

The two of them expressed their love for one another before Damien ran off and disappeared into the trees. Suddenly, Raphael stepped out from behind Tyson.

"Are you alright?" Raphael asked sympathetically.

"Yes, thank you," Harmony said cheerfully. She looked at her brother, hoping he believed her even though tears were beginning to form in her eyes.

Raphael walked up to his sister and put his arms around her. "Are you still going to compete?" he asked.

"Of course I am," Harmony said pushing her brother away. She could not believe her brother would have to ask.

The two of them walked back to the horsebox together with Harmony leading Tyson. When they arrived she quickly got Tyson ready to compete in the next round of the competition.

In the next round her rival fell off her horse, allowing Harmony to move on to the third round. In the semi-final Harmony was losing coming to the last fence. She had to hope the girl who was leading knocked the last fence down.

Harmony breathed a sigh of relief as her rival's horse ploughed through the fence, allowing her to compete in the final.

In the final, Harmony managed to get a good lead so all she had to do was hope that Tyson left all the jumps intact. Luckily for her, Tyson was in the mood for jumping so not one pole fell meaning Harmony had won the class. She patted Tyson and gave him a hug to let him know he had done well.

After being presented with the winner's prize, Harmony rode a lap of honour around the arena. As she gently kicked her heels to go faster Tyson started playing up. Harmony tried to calm him down enough to complete a circuit of the arena. Her attempts failed when he suddenly bolted out of the arena. He galloped straight past the horsebox where Goliath had just finished tacking up the other horses ready for all of them to go for a hack together.

As Harmony's horse carried on running, Goliath mounted Condor. He turned his horse ready to go after Harmony. Goliath caught a glimpse of Harmony just as Tyson took her to the patch of grass they had been in earlier.

When Tyson finally stopped in the area of grass, Harmony noticed Damien stood looking miserable. Harmony dismounted from her horse. Little did she know Goliath had followed her and he was now hiding in the trees watching.

Harmony turned to look at Tyson. "I guess you are okay with me and Damien being together," she said lovingly as she stroked him.

Harmony called out to Damien, who came running towards her and then held her in a warm embrace.

Goliath could not believe his eyes when he saw Harmony with a young man he did not recognise. Little did he know things were about to get worse. Damien gently moved Harmony's hair behind her ear to reveal her pointy ear, Harmony gently brushed Damien's hair behind his ear to reveal his human ear. Goliath was starting to wonder if he was really seeing what he was seeing. Was Harmony hugging a human? Harmony and Damien stood looking at each other lovingly. By this time Goliath had moved closer to them. He looked up just as Harmony and Damien started kissing.

Now that Condor had moved closer, Tyson could sense him in the trees. Tyson started moving around restlessly trying to warn Harmony by getting her attention.

Goliath kicked his horse into a canter and charged into the patch of grass. When Harmony heard the sound of hooves approaching she stepped back from Damien.

Goliath charged across the grass before stopping between Harmony and Damien. Both boys gazed hard at one another. "You are never to come near her again. Do I make myself clear?" Goliath warned him angrily.

Harmony stepped forward putting her hands on Goliath's knee. "Goliath, please, you cannot stop us from seeing each other. My mother would have let me if she was still here."

Goliath ignored her childish behaviour. "TYSON, COME HERE!" he shouted.

Tyson never moved, causing Goliath to shout again. This time Tyson slowly walked forward towards him. Goliath grabbed one of his reins before looking fixedly at Harmony. "Mount up," he ordered.

Harmony bowed her head. "As you wish, Prince Goliath," she said sarcastically.

Damien wanted to double check what he had just heard. "What did you just call him?" he asked.

"Be quiet, human," Goliath replied sternly.

Harmony mounted up not wanting to push Goliath's patience any further. Goliath got Condor to walk forward while he was leading Tyson. They had just got to the opening in the trees when Harmony suddenly pulled on one of Tyson's reins. The rein that Goliath had been holding was yanked out of his hand. Harmony turned Tyson and cantered back over to Damien.

Goliath chased after Harmony wanting to stop her reaching Damien. When he caught up with her, he turned Condor in front of Tyson. Harmony had to stop quickly so that she did not crash in to Condor. She was about to go out round the horse when three other horses surrounded her. She was now boxed in. Harmony looked up to see her father, her brother and her cousin looking at her.

"DAMIEN, RUN!" Harmony shouted, wanting to protect him from her family.

Damien started running across the grass. Harmony dismounted from Tyson wishing she could go to him.

Raphael turned his horse, Pandora, and went in hot pursuit of Damien.

"LEAVE HIM ALONE. I LOVE HIM!" Harmony shouted at her brother.

Raphael caught up with Damien easily. The two of them stopped. Raphael pulled back Damien's hair to reveal his ears. "He is a human," Raphael called back to the group.

They all looked down at Harmony, causing her to look nervously at the ground avoiding their gaze. "We have been in love since I was living with the humans," she admitted to her family.

Maurice turned to look at his son. "We will talk about this at home. Harmony, get on the back of your brother's horse," he ordered.

Harmony looked at her brother before turning to look at her father. "I would if Raphael was not already on her," she joked.

Maurice looked sternly at his daughter. "I want you to ride on the horse with your brother." He was already angry about the Damien situation, so Harmony's joke was not making things any better.

Goliath grabbed hold of Tyson's reins so that he could lead him back to the horsebox while Harmony was going to be on the back of her brother's horse so that she could not cause any more trouble.

Harmony looked sadly at Damien knowing her family would not let her see him again for a long time, if ever. She walked over to her brother making sure she did not make eye contact with Damien. Raphael gently helped his sister on to the back of his horse. Once everyone was ready to go they all rode off back to the horsebox.

CHAPTER NINE

Everyone got into the horsebox except for Maurice and Goliath, who had to load the horses into the horsebox.

Once everything had been put away, Goliath began the journey home. With the different emotions in the horsebox it made an uncomfortable atmosphere. To try and block out the different emotions, Harmony focused on listening to the horses.

Harmony stared out the window thinking about her human boyfriend. She sat hoping that one day she would get to see him again. Not only had she lost her mother, which she had found extremely hard to accept, but now she had to deal with losing Damien as well.

When they got home they all took care of their own horses to get the job done quicker. After taking care of the horses, everyone went back to the cottage. Once inside the cottage they all started arguing.

"I CANNOT BELIEVE YOU JUST DID THAT. I LOVE DAMIEN. NOTHING YOU SAY OR DO IS GOING TO CHANGE THAT!" Harmony shouted. Tears of heartbreak rolled down her cheeks.

Maurice firmly grabbed his daughter's wrists. "YOU LIED TO US. NOT TO MENTION THE FACT THAT HE IS A HUMAN!" he shouted back.

"In case you have forgotten, I lived with humans for years. I practically was one apart from the weird shaped ears," Harmony stated angrily. She was trying her hardest to break free from her father's grip.

Maurice freed his daughter's wrists, pushing her to the floor. Harmony looked up at her father with tears streaming from her eyes, trying to fight the sobs that were threatening to escape.

"WE, ARE, ELVES. What part of that do you not understand?" Maurice shouted.

There was silence while Harmony got up from the floor. She was just about to retaliate when an unexpected female voice started speaking. "Maybe you should give the girl a break, Maurice," the voice said calmly.

"Believe me I intend to, I have not decided where yet… her leg or her neck," he told her sounding serious, but Freedom knew he was joking.

"Remember, you have just told her that her mother has been dead for years," the voice told him.

Harmony turned around and screamed. "Oh, my god! Freedom, what are you doing here?" she asked cheerfully.

The two of them hugged.

"I came to see my best friend," Freedom said, pleased to see Harmony.

The boys left the room so that Harmony could speak to her friend alone. Once the room was empty the two girls stepped away from each other.

"I am so glad to see you. My family have been completely against me lately. Then today at the competition they told me that my mother has been dead for years. No warning just straight out with it. They also told me that I am no longer allowed to see Damien," Harmony complained.

"Why are they no longer letting you see Damien?" Freedom asked.

Harmony looked at her friend wondering if she really did not know the answer. "They do not like him because he is a human. You know what my father thinks about humans," she answered, as though she was stating the obvious.

Freedom put her arm around Harmony's shoulders. "Your father needs to understand that you have spent time with humans, so you are going to get along with them. I also think your father needs to calm down and relax more."

Maurice entered the room to get the newspaper. "Careful, Freedom. Your family may be landed gentry, but right now you are just like any other young lady in my cottage," he warned her after hearing their conversation.

After picking up the newspaper he left the room, leaving the two girls alone.

Harmony let out a deep sigh of relief before returning to her conversation with Freedom. "I agree. The only problem is, as long as I want to mix with humans he will be under pressure from the elves because of the rules against humans, causing him to put pressure on me," Harmony explained.

"I know. That is why I think you need to get away from here for a while. I would suggest you take Goliath, he could take you to Elvesbridge to mix with the other elves. Lots of elves spend time in the main town. It might get your family off your back," Freedom suggested.

Harmony looked at her friend. "I think that is a great idea. There is just one problem. What if I fall in love with an elf?"

Freedom withdrew her arm from Harmony's shoulders, surprised by her question. It made her wonder if there was a reason for the question, perhaps she had already fallen in love with an elf and wanted to know what to do with the situation she was now facing.

Harmony walked away, processing the thought of maybe betraying Damien. The current expression on her face allowed Freedom to know what she was thinking.

"All I can say is, just let it happen; you cannot help what you feel for someone," Freedom answered reassuringly.

Harmony knew at that moment she did not want to go to town with Goliath, she would rather go with her friend. She turned to Freedom, "I have had an idea. You know Elvesbridge, so why don't you come with me rather than Goliath?" Harmony asked.

Freedom did not want to hurt her friend's feelings, but she was unsure of Harmony's plan for her to go to town instead of Goliath. "I would love to come with you," she answered trying to sound pleased with the invite.

Harmony walked over to the door. "Shall we get going," she said enthusiastically. She was starting to sound excited with the trip.

Freedom walked over to Harmony. "We had better let Goliath know where we are going."

"Why do we need to tell Goliath?" Harmony asked.

"I would feel happier if we let him know that we are going out," Freedom replied.

The two of them went to find Goliath. When they found him, he was sat at the kitchen table reading the newspaper. The two girls entered the kitchen, therefore Goliath put his newspaper down on the table. Harmony made her way over to the kitchen sink to look out the window into the garden, as she did not want to look at Goliath.

"Can we talk for a moment?" Freedom asked.

"Sure," Goliath said.

Freedom sat across the table from Goliath. "I am taking Harmony to Elvesbridge."

Goliath looked at Harmony before looking back at Freedom. "You are taking her to Elvesbridge?" he asked surprised, and then started laughing at the idea.

"What is so funny about that?" Freedom asked curiously.

"Well, she spent so much time with humans and now everyone expects her to just fit straight back in. The other elves know that she has spent time with humans so they will probably react just as her father has."

Freedom leaned forward so that her arms were resting on the table. "That does not matter. They will realise that she is trying to change. Unlike you, they will hopefully give her a chance," Freedom responded unconvincingly.

From her friend's tone of voice, Harmony knew that if she was not in the room, Freedom would be agreeing with Goliath. She also decided she had had enough of them talking like she was not there. "Hey, you two. I am stood here you know," she told them disgusted by the way they had treated her.

"Just ignore them," a voice said from the boot room.

The three of them looked up to see Rhoda stood in the doorway. Rhoda walked over to the sink where Harmony was still standing. "If you get up early tomorrow we will go to Elvesbridge together," she offered.

"Are you sure?" Harmony asked.

"Of course, that will then leave those two free to carry on their love fest," Rhoda replied.

Harmony smiled. "Thank you," she told her cousin.

"Well I had better be going or Amos will be wondering where I am," Rhoda informed them. She left the kitchen through the backdoor, leaving Harmony alone with Freedom and Goliath.

Goliath looked up at Harmony. "Your cousin must be mad to take you to Elvesbridge tomorrow."

"Why do you think that?" Harmony asked trying to remain calm.

"Come on, Harmony. Even you have got to admit that you do not fit in here. You are not like an elf in any way, Goliath said.

"Well guess what, Prince Goliath. I don't care what you or any of the other elves think about me. I am who I am and they will just have to get used to it," Harmony said confidently. She then walked out of the cottage to find her brother.

CHAPTER TEN

Now that Harmony was on her own she started to feel hurt by what Goliath and Freedom had said about her in the kitchen. After walking through the back garden, Harmony eventually found her brother at the stable-yard.

When Raphael heard someone behind him he turned around. As soon as he saw his sister he could clearly see she was upset so he quickly made his way over to her. "What is wrong?" he asked concerned.

Harmony looked up at her brother. Even before she spoke, tears were filling her eyes. "It is just something Goliath said to Freedom in the house."

She walked over to one of the stables then started stroking the grey horse that was inside. She turned her head to look at her brother. "Do you think I am meant to be living here, with the elves?" she asked.

Raphael was slightly confused by his sister's question. "Of course you are. You belong here as much as anyone," he answered, putting his arm around her shoulders.

"Thanks. You always say the right things. You are also the best brother anyone could hope for," she told him.

Raphael stood thinking about everything his sister had just said to him. "Who told you that you do not belong here?" he asked.

"No one really, it was just the way they said it. Freedom told Goliath that she was taking me to Elvesbridge. He then started laughing at the idea. He said that everyone expects me to fit in. Freedom then pretty much started agreeing with him." Harmony was getting more and more upset as she told her brother what they had said to each other.

"I am just going to ride out on Pandora. Why don't you come with me? You could ride Blizzard as he has not been out in a while," Raphael said.

"That sounds great," Harmony replied.

Raphael had already got Pandora in from the field. Blizzard was still in his stable after being put in that morning for breakfast. The two of them spent quite a bit of time getting the horses ready for the ride. Raphael never spoke as he knew that was how his sister liked to work.

Once the horses were ready, they set off on their journey across the open fields. The horses enjoyed it as they got to race across the fields. On the ride they also encountered a stony lane to ride along. Harmony chose to take the opportunity to talk to her brother some more. They rode side by side to be able to hear each other more clearly.

"You know what," Harmony said thoughtfully.

"What?" Raphael asked.

"One thing I would love to do would be to ride the horses on the beach. Maybe even in the sea," Harmony answered looking at the sky.

Raphael smiled. He then nodded, pleased with his idea. "I will take you with a couple of the horses to the beach. We can ride on the sand and maybe in the sea," Raphael told her.

"When are we going to do it?" Harmony asked excitedly.

"We can go tomorrow as long as nothing else comes up," Raphael said.

"Tomorrow I am going to town with Rhoda," she reminded him.

"How about we go at the weekend?" he asked.

"That sounds good," she said smiling.

Raphael was pleased to see his sister smiling. "I am glad that I have made you happy."

After riding along the lane, the two of them came to more fields. The two of them stopped in the first field. After Raphael closed the gate, Harmony twisted round in the saddle to face her brother. "I will race you home," she told him. She never gave her brother a chance to say anything, and before he knew it, his sister was charging off across the field. Raphael kicked Pandora into a gallop to try to catch up to her, but Blizzard was a very fast horse, which made it difficult for Pandora to catch up.

When Harmony got to the track, she stopped to wait for her brother. Harmony and Raphael slowly walked the horses along the track to the stableyard. When they got back to the stables, Harmony's other cousin was there.

"What are you doing here?" Raphael asked, although he had a good idea as to why she was there.

"Maurice told me that Harmony needed help settling back into elvish life," Leander answered.

Raphael and Harmony both dismounted from their horses.

"That is it. I am going to kill our father," Harmony shouted angrily. She put Blizzard in his stable before storming off to the cottage.

Harmony burst in through the backdoor of the cottage. She found her father sat at the dining table. "I cannot believe you. I am adjusting just fine. I do not need you to keep sending people to help me."

Maurice put his pen down next to a load of papers. "If that is how you would like it. You can carry on being miserable," he said angrily.

Harmony moved over to the dining table. "Thanks to Rhoda and my brother I am not miserable anymore. They are doing a better job than anyone."

"As your brother, he should want to make you happy," Maurice stated as a matter of fact.

Harmony pushed away from the table then she stood by the sink. "At least he is doing something, which is a lot more than you are doing. Today he invited me to go on a ride with him, letting me ride Blizzard. He has also offered to take me to the beach with the horses," Harmony said calmly.

During the first shouting match, Raphael had walked in to give his sister some backup. "Harmony is right. What have you done, Father, apart from getting other people to help her. People who have ended up upsetting her."

Maurice stood up. "I know what is best for my daughter," he said angrily.

Raphael turned his back on his father.

"I have stood by her ever since she got back," Maurice added confidently.

Hardly able to believe what he was hearing, Raphael turned sharply to face his father. "You have not stood by her, that is my point. You have asked old friends and family to help her adjust to elvish life, while you sat back and watched how unhappy your daughter was," he exclaimed.

"Can you please stop arguing?" Harmony shouted.

Raphael and Maurice looked at Harmony. While they had been arguing they had both forgotten she was stood in the kitchen.

"I am sorry, Harmony," Raphael apologised.

Harmony moved over to the table. "Look, maybe Goliath had a point. I am not supposed to be here. I belong with the humans," she told them.

Maurice looked sternly at his daughter. "I will not let you leave," he told her.

"You have no choice, Father. You have ruined my life once, please do not do it again."

Raphael walked over to his sister. "Come on, Harmony. I think you need to calm down for a little while."

"I don't need to calm down. I need to disown this family!" Harmony shouted and then ran off to the stable-yard. As Blizzard was in his stable she decided to sit next to the stable door.

Back in the house Raphael had become really angry with his father. Raphael whipped round to face his father after watching Harmony run out of the backdoor. "YOU SEE WHAT YOU HAVE DONE. YOU CALL THAT YOUR DAUGHTER BEING HAPPY!" he shouted out in anger.

"She walked away from me. She also has a temper," Maurice said.

Raphael turned away from his father in disgust. He then faced his father once again. "OH, MY GOSH, WHEN ARE YOU GOING TO GET YOUR HEAD OUT OF YOUR BACKSIDE AND START CARING FOR YOUR FAMILY?" He was still shouting as he could not believe how blind his father was being to the situation.

"I do care about my family. It is just that... I never wanted a daughter. I had only wanted sons... sons who would become protectors of Elveshire," Maurice explained quietly so that no one would overhear.

Raphael was stunned into silence. It took him a minute to absorb what his father had just told him. "True, although girls can become patrol riders for the royal family. She could do it just like Mother did," Raphael told him.

Maurice looked down at the table to avoid making eye contact with his son. "I did not want it to happen again."

"You did not want what to happen again?" Raphael asked confused.

"You had better sit down; this could be hard for you to hear," Maurice told him.

Raphael sat down slowly in the chair next to his father. He could not understand what his father meant about it not happening again. Once Raphael was sat comfortably, he focused on what his father was about to tell him.

Maurice looked up at his son. "Your mother was selected to be a patrol rider. One day the royal family were out on parade, and your mother was riding with them. The parade had been going well until your mother's horse got scared. The horse started throwing itself about trying to get her off its back. She was such a good rider that she managed to stay on. Then the unexpected happened." He paused to compose himself for the next part of the story.

"What happened?" Raphael asked eagerly.

"The horse reared up so high that it fell over backwards with your mother still on its back. They managed to get the horse off her quite quickly. Although the horse was fine, your mother was not. She had broken bones as well as some damage to her internal organs."

"Where did you take her?"

"I was so scared of losing your mother that I broke the rules and took her to a human hospital. I was hoping that they could save her, which I knew the elves had no chance of doing."

"Did it work?" Raphael asked.

"The doctors did the best they could, but it was not enough. They came over to me and told me that she was slowly dying. Once I had got her home I never let her out of my sight. You and your sister were only little when it happened," Maurice explained sadly.

Raphael was trying his hardest not to cry. "Is that when Harmony went to live with the humans?" he asked.

Maurice straightened up in his chair as he found this topic easier to talk about. "With your mother unable to do anything I started to struggle. Without you or your mother knowing, I took Harmony to the humans. I left her on a doorstep with a blanket wrapped around her shoulders. After I came back it took your mother a day to realise Harmony had gone. She wanted desperately to go and visit her. It hurt her so much that she could not go. When Harmony never came to see her, your mother began to go downhill rapidly. It was about a month later when your mother was gone. It hit me so hard I decided to leave your sister where she was. I felt it best for her."

Raphael could not fight the sadness anymore. He wiped the tears away from his eyes, not wanting his father to see him crying. "Where did Mother think Harmony had gone?" he asked.

"She thought that Harmony had gone to stay with a friend," Maurice replied.

"What horse was Mother riding in the parade?"

Maurice went to touch his son's hand, but Raphael quickly pulled his hands off the table. "The horse was called Pride," Maurice said.

Raphael sat for a moment trying to think if the name sounded familiar. "How come I know that name?" he asked still deep in thought.

Maurice got up from his chair. "The name sounds familiar because Blizzard is Pride's full brother," he said.

Raphael got up from his chair then Maurice walked off into the living room.

CHAPTER ELEVEN

Raphael decided to go and find his sister. He walked out of the backdoor into the back garden. He had just started walking along the path when he spotted Harmony sat on the swing bench. Raphael crossed the grass to get to the bench. He sat down next to his sister, remaining silent. Harmony slowly looked up at her brother. As she looked at him Raphael could tell his sister had been crying. He decided to try cheering her up by discussing their trip the next day. "Rhoda and Amos are picking us up at about half seven in the morning," he informed her.

Harmony smiled. Even though she was not looking forward to doing any shopping, she was looking forward to spending time with her cousins and brother. "That sounds good. I was thinking of sleeping in the horsebox tonight."

"Why would you do that?" Raphael asked.

"I wanted to keep out of Father's way," she replied.

"You should not let him push you out of the house," he said, and then got up from the swing bench and held his hand out to his sister. "Shall we go back to the cottage?"

Harmony took hold of her brother's hand as she got up and they embraced one another before making their way back to the cottage.

The two of them quietly entered the kitchen, hoping their father would not be sat at the table. Raphael walked in closely followed by Harmony. They were pleased to find the kitchen empty. Knowing their father would be in the living room, the siblings crept along the hallway not wanting to acknowledge him, then went straight to their bedrooms.

Harmony entered her bedroom then walked over to her window seat and sat looking at the view. As it was getting dark, Harmony could not see much so she opened her window to look at the stars coming out. She felt happy looking at the stars, it felt like all her troubles were floating off into the darkness.

Once Harmony felt relaxed she shut her window and curtains. She changed into her nightwear then climbed in to bed. For the first time in a long time she had a good night's sleep.

The next morning Harmony woke up to see it was still dark outside. She rolled over to look at her clock, hoping it was early enough to be able to go back to sleep. When she looked at the clock she saw that it was time to get up. Not wanting to get out of bed, she slipped her feet out one by one before sitting up.

Carefully getting to her feet she walked to the bathroom where she had a wash. On the way back to her bedroom she looked over at her brother's door to find it still shut. Harmony guessed he was still in bed.

After walking back into her room Harmony walked over to her wardrobe to choose an outfit to wear for the day. As she looked at her clothes she realised none of them were going to be acceptable amongst the elves; her only options were her riding clothes or her human clothes.

It was a cold day, and as a result, Harmony decided on a pair of bootleg jeans with a long purple top and a pair of ankle boots. Once she had her outfit picked out she took it over to her bed ready for her to get dressed. After Harmony had put her clothes on she walked over to her chest of drawers where she put on a black choker with a matching bracelet. She wanted to put on some makeup but decided to tone it down a bit from what she would normally wear.

Leaving her bedroom, Harmony went downstairs to get some breakfast. She walked into the empty kitchen where she made breakfast before taking it to the table to eat alone.

Not knowing how long her brother was going to be, she put the milk in the fridge before sitting back down at the table to eat her breakfast alone. She had not been eating for long when her brother entered the kitchen.

"Good morning," Raphael said.

"Good morning," Harmony returned.

Raphael got a spoon and bowl before getting the milk out of the fridge before joining his sister at the table.

"What are we going to Elvesbridge for?" Harmony asked.

"As you are going to be living here permanently now we need to turn you in to a true elf, starting with the clothes," Raphael answered. He ate a spoonful of cereal then looked at his sister again. "Speaking of which, is that what you are wearing?"

"It was the best I could do," Harmony replied looking down at her clothes.

She took her bowl over to the sink then went back to the table to get the milk. She put the milk away before washing up her breakfast things. "How are we getting to Elvesbridge?" she asked.

"Amos and Rhoda are going to pick us up in the cart."

"How long have we got until they get here?"

"Not long," Raphael said, getting up from the table to take his bowl and spoon to his sister. "Why do you ask?" he asked, handing her his bowl and spoon.

"Now that I am going to become an elf permanently I want to enjoy these last few moments of feeling like a human," Harmony replied as she took the bowl and spoon from her brother.

Raphael started drying up the breakfast things that Harmony had washed up. "So you have decided to be a member of the elves?" Raphael asked.

"I am actually hoping that Father will talk to me if I make the effort to be more like you," Harmony answered.

With all the breakfast things put away, the two of them walked out the front door to wait for Rhoda and Amos. They sat on the doorstep side by side then just waited.

While they were sat waiting, Raphael looked at Harmony. "You really want to get along with Father, don't you?" he asked.

"Yes, I do. I just do not know what I have done wrong to make him treat me the way he does," Harmony said.

Raphael looked away from his sister. "I am sure he will come around eventually," he reassured her.

The two of them were sat in silence when they heard a horse and cart approaching the cottage. Raphael and Harmony looked up to see Amos and Rhoda approaching in a cart pulled by their two palomino horses. Amos stopped the cart in front of Raphael and Harmony.

"Are you two ready to go?" Rhoda asked.

Raphael got up from the step first.

"I guess so," Harmony replied, slowly getting up from the step.

Raphael climbed on the cart first before helping his sister up. Once everyone was seated, the four of them set off for Elvesbridge.

During the journey Rhoda looked at Harmony before looking at Raphael. "You are letting her wear that to town?" she asked.

Raphael looked at Rhoda. "It was the best she could do," he said.

"Amos, stop the cart please," Rhoda instructed.

Amos pulled over as his sister had instructed. She got down from the front of the cart to walk round to the back. Rhoda climbed up then told Harmony to stand up. She lifted the seat before pulling out a cloak which she handed to Harmony. "Put that cloak over the top of your clothes so the elves cannot see them," she instructed.

Harmony took her coat off which she handed to Rhoda before putting the cloak over her clothes. While Harmony was putting the cloak on, Rhoda put the coat away under the seat. Once Harmony had the cloak on she sat back down. Rhoda rejoined her brother in the front then they set off again.

"What have we got to do in town?" Rhoda asked.

"You have got a lot to do," Raphael answered grinning.

"Like what?" Rhoda asked. She turned to look at her cousin.

"Well, there is money, dresses, underwear and shoes," Raphael answered.

Harmony looked up at the others. "So, you three are just going to torture me all day," she complained.

"Yes we are," the others replied at the same time.

After they had been travelling for a bit longer Harmony was beginning to get bored. "Are we there yet?" she asked.

"Nearly there," Amos answered.

"Why? Are you excited about going shopping?" Raphael asked.

"No. The sooner we get there the sooner this nightmare will be over," Harmony replied.

After that no one spoke until they arrived at the town stables. The horses would be spending the day there while the others went shopping.

Harmony and Raphael climbed down from the back of the cart while Rhoda climbed down from the front. The three of them stood waiting outside while Amos took the horses into the stables.

When he joined them outside they all walked to the bank where Harmony could get some money out of her bank account. Raphael handed his sister her bank book before following her inside. Harmony looked around at the inside of the bank as the two of them made their way over to the short queue. To her surprise the elves' bank was just like a human bank.

After looking around, Harmony turned to her brother. "How much money should I take out?" she asked.

"I think a few hundred should be enough," Raphael said.

While they were in the queue Harmony could see that some of the elves were looking at her. Luckily it was not long before it was Harmony's turn. She had her bank book updated before taking out the money she would need.

As they left, Raphael put the book and money into a satchel-type bag he had. When they got outside, two girls had joined Rhoda and Amos.

"What is going on?" Harmony asked, confused by the appearance of the two strangers.

"You are going shopping with Rhoda and her two friends," Raphael replied.

"What are you and Amos going to be doing?" Harmony asked.

"We are going to be meeting up with a couple of friends," Raphael said.

Rhoda walked over to Harmony, so her friends followed.

Raphael handed Harmony the bag with her bank book and money in before turning to Rhoda. "Now it is your turn to take charge for the clothes shopping. You may find you need to use a bit of force to get her to buy things," he told her.

"Okay, time to go shopping," Rhoda instructed.

Harmony reluctantly walked away with Rhoda and her friends. She looked round just as her brother and cousin were walking off in the opposite direction. As the group of girls approached the first shop, Harmony noticed her pull a piece of paper out of the little pouch she was carrying.

Rhoda looked up at Harmony. "I made a list of everything we need to get," she informed her.

The first shop they came to was a dress shop. Rhoda's friends walked into the shop first followed by Rhoda then a reluctant Harmony. Rhoda stopped next to the first rail of dresses before looking at Harmony. "What dress size are you?" she asked.

"A medium I think," Harmony replied.

"Okay, so pick out a dress in a medium size then try it on to see if it fits," Rhoda instructed.

Harmony looked down at the dresses on the rail next to her, thinking she had stepped back in time to the early twentieth century. She found a dress in a medium size then picked it up. Rhoda followed her to the fitting rooms while her friends carried on looking at the dresses. Harmony tried on the dress then came out of the fitting room to show Rhoda.

"At least now we know we need to be looking for dresses in a medium size," Rhoda told her.

Harmony went back into the fitting room to take the dress off. Rhoda waited for her to come out so that they could start choosing some dresses. While Rhoda was waiting for Harmony to get dressed, her friends walked over to her.

"Did that dress fit?" Daisy asked.

"Yes, it did. Now all we need to do is find dresses that Harmony likes," Rhoda replied.

"That is not going to be easy," Harmony said as she came out the fitting room.

"Why not?" Daisy asked.

"I do not like dresses," Harmony said.

The girls started looking at the dresses on the rails. Harmony had only chosen a couple of dresses, leaving it up to Rhoda and her friends to choose the rest. By the time they were done they had got at least ten dresses. Some of them were short-sleeved for summer, the others were long-sleeved for winter.

After paying for the dresses, Harmony joined her cousin and her friends. "Where are we going next?" she asked.

"We are going to get nightwear and your undergarments," Rhoda said.

"My what?" Harmony asked, surprised by what her cousin had said.

"You will need a corset, some bloomers and some chemises," Rhoda said.

The four girls walked along the street heading towards the next shop. On the way, Rhoda spotted Harmony watching three young men.

"Who are those three good looking guys?" Harmony asked.

"They are Goliath's younger brothers," Rhoda answered.

Harmony quickly turned her head to look at Rhoda. "No way are they related to Goliath. They seem so nice," she said in disbelief.

Harmony was still thinking about the three brothers when the girls walked into the nightwear shop. The lady in the shop walked over to the girls. "Hello. How may I help you?"

"My cousin Harmony has a list of items that she needs," Rhoda said.

"What is on the list?" the lady asked.

"Four pairs of bloomers, a selection of chemises and a few corsets," Rhoda replied.

The lady walked behind the counter to grab a tape measure. "Okay, Harmony, if you would like to follow me we will get you measured."

Harmony followed the lady to the fitting room.

While Harmony was gone, Rhoda took the opportunity to talk to her friends. "What do you think of Harmony?" she asked.

"I do not think we have got to know the real Harmony yet. The only thing we know about her is that she does not like shopping," Summer said.

"We also know that she likes three of Goliath's brothers," Daisy added.

"I thought it was going to be hard to get Harmony to forget about her human boyfriend but after the way she looked at Goliath's brothers, it gives me hope," Rhoda told them.

Not long after the girls' conversation had ended, Harmony rejoined them.

"How did it go?" Rhoda asked.

"It was a nightmare. I cannot wait to get this shopping trip over and done with," Harmony replied.

The four of them stood waiting in silence while the shop assistant grabbed Harmony what she needed. Rhoda walked over to the door to wait with her friends for Harmony. Once Harmony paid for everything they all left the shop.

"Where are we going next?" Summer asked.

"We are going to the shoe shop," Rhoda replied.

Harmony smiled. "Now shoes I can deal with," she told them.

As they were making their way to the last shop, Amos and Raphael caught up with them. Rhoda stopped so that she could update them on their shopping progress.

"Have you got much more left to do?" Raphael asked.

"Just the shoe shop, then we will be done," Rhoda replied.

"Amos and I will head over to the stables and get the horses ready to leave. We will meet you over there," Raphael informed her.

Rhoda nodded in agreement, and then she walked with the girls to the shoe shop. As the girls approached the shop, Rhoda asked Harmony, "What shoe size are you?"

"I am a size four."

Rhoda walked into the shoe shop with her friends and started picking out shoes for Harmony to try on. While waiting for Rhoda, Summer and Daisy to pick out shoes, Harmony sat down on one of the stools, wishing she was at the stables with Tyson. She was not going to get the opportunity that afternoon as she had chores to do in the cottage.

After trying on lots of shoes, Rhoda finally picked out four pairs for Harmony to buy. After purchasing the shoes, the girls left the final shop.

"Are we going home now?" Harmony asked.

"Yes, we are," Rhoda said.

Harmony walked towards the town stables with her bags of shopping. She felt so happy to find that the horses and cart were ready to go. She quickly put the shopping in the cart before climbing aboard. Rhoda put the rest of the bags in before saying thank you and goodbye to her friends. Rhoda climbed aboard so they began the journey back home.

"So, Harmony, what do you think of Elvesbridge?" Raphael asked.

"It is not too bad; it is just quiet. It also feels like I have stepped back in history. All the buildings look Tudor style."

"What do you mean?" Raphael asked.

"I mean here everyone seems to go to town for a reason. No one just goes to town for fun."

"We are always busy with all our other jobs to go to town for fun," Rhoda informed her.

Harmony knew the jobs her cousin meant because she now had to do them as well.

CHAPTER TWELVE

The journey home did not take as long because they did not need to stop. When they arrived at Harmony's house Raphael helped his sister out of the cart with her shopping. They all said goodbye to each other before Amos and Rhoda carried on their journey home.

Raphael passed Harmony her shopping bags before opening the front door. He walked in followed by Harmony. Once she had entered the cottage, Harmony took her shopping straight up to her bedroom. Raphael walked into the living room where his father was sat in his chair.

"After seeing the effort Harmony put into today I think you should go and talk to her. Maybe even make up with her," Raphael advised.

Maurice looked up at his son. "I think you are right, son. Thank you," he said.

Maurice left the living room to go to his daughter's bedroom. He knocked on the door then waited to be invited in.

"Come in," Harmony said.

Maurice entered the bedroom where he found his daughter sat looking out her bedroom window. "Can I talk to you for a moment?" he asked.

"Of course."

Maurice looked at the shopping bags she had got that morning which were on her bed. He walked across the room before sitting next to his daughter on her window seat. "What has been bothering you?" he asked, trying to sound concerned.

Harmony looked up at her father, surprised that he was even asking that question. She turned to look back out the window before answering: "I just wish I knew how Mother died." She had not expected to be able to talk to her father so easily.

"I can tell you that," he said.

Harmony perked up slightly, glad that she was finally going to hear the truth about her mother's death. "You can. Well, how did she die?" she asked.

Maurice looked out the window, not wanting to look at his daughter while he explained what happened. "She was terminally ill after a horse riding accident," he said.

Harmony turned her head so that she was also looking out the window. "I am going to ride even more now to make up for the times that Mother could not," she told her father.

Maurice turned to look at his daughter. "I know a way that you can make your mother proud of you," he informed her.

"Really, what is it?" Harmony asked eagerly.

"You could become a patrol rider for the royal family. We will help you prepare for the try-outs."

Harmony got up from the window seat. "If you tell me how I will need to ride I can come up with ways to practise," she said, sounding determined.

"Who are you planning on riding?" Maurice asked.

Harmony had to think for a minute. "I think I will ride Blizzard."

Maurice got up from the window seat. "That is a good choice. There is not much you need to do to improve your riding... you have the same calmness as your mother did when you ride. The only problem you have is you need to deepen your seat. Think more like a dressage rider instead of a show jumper."

Harmony looked at her father while wondering why he wanted to help her. "Thank you for wanting to help me. I know exactly how to solve my problem. I will ride Blizzard in the paddock with no stirrups," she explained.

Maurice smiled at his daughter. "The try-outs are in a week, therefore we will really need to work hard to be ready in time. I thought that in a minute maybe you could tack Blizzard up and ride him in the paddock to work on your seat. Then tomorrow you, Raphael, Amos and I could ride around together."

Harmony nodded in agreement. "This afternoon will give me a good opportunity to ride without stirrups."

Maurice walked over to the door. "As you know the horses, I will let you decide who we ride," he informed her, and then left the room so that Harmony could change into her riding clothes.

Before getting changed she looked out of her window at the horses. She thought about it for a few minutes before finally deciding who was going to ride who. Once the decision had been made, Harmony got changed so that she could get down to the stableyard.

CHAPTER THIRTEEN

When Harmony got to the stable-yard, Blizzard was in the field. She got his head-collar from the tack room before going to the field to fetch him. As she got to the field she noticed that all the horses were in the lower part of the field except for two. Blizzard and Bluebell had decided to stay furthest away from the gate.

Harmony put Blizzard's head-collar on and then started to head for the gate. As she started to walk, something pulled on her arm. She turned around to find Blizzard refusing to move. Harmony pulled on the rope hoping to get him to move but he just kept pulling in the opposite direction. After about half an hour she finally managed to get him to the gate.

Once they were through the gate Harmony led him to the stable-yard to get him ready to go to the sand school. She quickly brushed him over before tacking him up. She was just about to go to the sand school when somebody walked up behind her.

"Good afternoon, Harmony."

Harmony turned around to see Goliath stood there. "What are you doing here?" she asked.

"I came to see your father to see how you were doing and he told me about the patrol rider try-outs. He then informed me that you were out here practising."

"I am just about to start. Maybe you could coach me?" she asked.

"Okay, let us get started," he replied.

Harmony finished doing up Blizzard's girth then took his head-collar off. Goliath gave Harmony a leg up, then they made their way to the sand school.

Goliath watched as Harmony rode Blizzard around, slowly warming him up. While she was riding around, Goliath watched hoping that she would become a patrol rider. He snapped out of his thoughts when he noticed Harmony riding Blizzard towards him.

After riding around for a while, Harmony wanted Goliath's opinion on what he saw. "So, what do you think?" she asked.

Goliath took hold of Harmony's hand. "I think I am looking at a new patrol rider. I also think with a bit more work you could possibly be head patrol rider," he replied.

"Do you really think so?" Harmony asked, pleased with the report.

Goliath looked her in the eye. "I really do," he replied. He let go of Harmony's hand and then walked over to the gate to let her out.

Harmony rode Blizzard back to the yard before dismounting. She took the horse's bridle off before putting his head-collar on. She then handed the bridle to Goliath. "Can you get me his grooming kit please?" she asked as she handed him the bridle.

Goliath took the bridle from Harmony before making his way to the tack room. He put the bridle on the correct hook then picked up Blizzard's grooming kit. He carried the grooming kit out to the stable-yard where Harmony stood waiting for him. He put it down next to the stable and then looked at Harmony. "I am going to talk to your father," he informed her, and then walked off, leaving Harmony to put Blizzard to bed.

As it was Raphael's turn to put the horses to bed, Harmony only had Blizzard to see to allowing her to take her time with him. She placed him in his stable with his rug on before standing with the horse for a while, stroking him.

When it started to get to cold, Harmony decided to return to the cottage. As she walked through the backdoor her father was just putting the tea on the table. The warmth of the kitchen together with the lovely smell of stew was a welcome sight for Harmony after getting cold at the stables.

"After you have had tea, I think you should head to bed as it is going to be an early start tomorrow," he advised her.

The three family members sat at the dining table together in silence while they ate their tea. Her father seemed happy, so Harmony guessed that Goliath had spoken to him. For once Harmony felt as happy as she could because she felt like she belonged with the elves.

Raphael looked at his sister, then his father, wondering what could have happened to make the two of them become happy all of a sudden. He liked them being happy as it meant he did not have to play peacemaker between the two of them. "Why are you two happy all of a sudden?" he asked.

"No reason," Harmony said as she got up from her chair. She walked over to the sink and placed her plate in it. "I am off to bed," she informed them as she walked to the kitchen doorway.

"Goodnight," Maurice said.

"Goodnight," Raphael said also.

"Goodnight," Harmony said before leaving. She walked up to her bedroom, quickly getting changed then climbing into bed snuggling up under the covers.

Harmony could hear her family moving about downstairs in the kitchen. She then heard them leave to go to the stables. While the cottage was quiet, Harmony tried her best to fall asleep.

When Maurice and Raphael came back from the stable-yard they were quiet, hoping not to wake Harmony up if she was asleep. Raphael went into the living room with his father to warm up by the fire. Maurice sat in his chair and picked up a book. Raphael sat on the sofa to read. He picked up his book then looked at his father. "What was Goliath doing here earlier?" he asked.

Maurice closed his book before looking at his son. "I wanted to get his opinion on whether he thinks Harmony has what it takes to become a patrol rider," he said.

"What did he think?" Raphael asked.

"He thinks she could be a patrol rider."

The two of them went back to reading their books. After about half an hour Raphael put his book down ready to go to bed. He said goodnight to his father before quietly walking up the stairs because Harmony was already in bed. He went into his bedroom closing the door behind him.

CHAPTER FOURTEEN

The next morning, Harmony woke up to a sunny crisp morning. She pulled the covers tighter up under her chin to keep out the cold. She was lying looking towards her window when there was a knock at the door.

"Come on, Harmony. Time to get up," her brother called out to her.

Harmony heard him walk away from the door so she slowly got out of bed. As it was feeling quite cold out she decided to put an extra layer of clothing under her riding clothes. She got dressed before going to the bathroom to have a wash, and then went downstairs for breakfast.

In the kitchen, Raphael and Maurice had already started eating their breakfast. Harmony sat down at the table grabbing herself some toast. She listened to her father rattle the pages of the newspaper as he turned them, waiting for him to find some news he disagreed with.

Raphael finished eating first. Maurice followed closely behind leaving Harmony sat alone at the table to finish her breakfast. The two of them made their way into the living room to wait for her. When Harmony finished, she cleared the table before heading to the lounge. She walked in and then joined her brother on the sofa.

"We are just waiting for one more person then we will begin," Maurice informed them.

"Who are we waiting for?" Harmony asked, hoping it was not Goliath.

"Amos agreed to help us out," Maurice said.

The three of them were sat in the living room waiting in silence. They had not been sat there long when Amos appeared in the doorway. "Hello," he said as he entered the room.

Amos sat on the floor by Harmony's feet. Maurice sat forward in his chair ready to talk to everyone. "As Harmony knows the horses, I have decided to let her choose who we will ride," he told them.

They looked at Harmony waiting to find out who they would be riding. Harmony looked at everyone already knowing who was riding who. "I want Raphael to ride Tyson, Father to ride Romany, and Amos to ride Rosie," she informed them.

Now that they knew who they would be riding, they left the living room to go to the boot room. After they had put their riding boots on and grabbed their hats they walked together to the stable-yard.

"After what Goliath told me yesterday, I want to aim for head patrol rider," Harmony told them.

When they got to the stables the horses were still inside from the night before. They got the horses out of the stables and tied them up outside, ready for grooming. Not wanting to waste time, the horses were quickly brushed before being tacked up.

Raphael fell slightly behind as he had trouble picking up Tyson's feet to pick them out. He stood tugging on the horse's legs, not wanting to be defeated. In the end he had to call his sister over to lift the horse's feet. Harmony only had to touch Tyson's leg and he picked his foot up.

As soon as all the horses were ready, everyone mounted up. Harmony decided to start off by riding in the sand school with no stirrups. They followed each other single file round to the sand school where Harmony had been practising the day before. When they got to the gate Maurice opened it so that everyone could enter the school.

"I would like us all to line up side-by-side against the bottom fence. We will then ride from one end to the other. First, we will try it in walk before trying it in trot. If Blizzard behaves himself, we will then attempt a canter," Maurice instructed.

They all lined up next to each other against the bottom fence. Harmony was still riding without stirrups during the test. Blizzard had no trouble with the challenge in walk and trot. The problems started when they moved on to canter. He was not happy with the speed of the other horses causing Harmony to keep fighting with him to stop him from racing ahead. They finished the workout with a lap of walking around the edge of the sand school to cool the horses off before calling it a day.

"We will put the horses out in the field for the day," Maurice said.

They walked quietly back to the stables where everyone dismounted. Harmony put Blizzard in his stable to make untacking him easier. After all the horses had been untacked, they took them to the field where the horses would be spending the rest of the day. Once all the horses were in the field Maurice walked over to Harmony.

"Raphael and I have got to go to work so I would like you to clean up our stables," Maurice told her.

Harmony nodded to tell her father that she would do it and thought of the other jobs she had to do that day. The boys handed Harmony the horses' bridles before heading off to work. She walked back to the stable-yard to find the horses' saddles still on their stable doors.

"Thanks a lot, guys," Harmony mumbled to herself as she picked up the saddle closest to her. She ended up making a few trips to the tack room before all the tack was put away.

The next job for Harmony to tackle was the mucking out. She took all the hay-nets out of the stables before taking them round to the hay-barn. She next took all the water buckets out of the stables and lined them up by the outside tap. As she started walking back towards the first stable Goliath appeared.

"Hello, Harmony. I thought you would have been practising for try-outs," he said.

"Trust me, I wish I was, but father and Raphael are at work leaving me to do this instead," she said.

"I could help," Goliath offered.

"How would you do that?" Harmony asked curiously.

"I could do the mucking out while you are practising."

"Are you sure?"

"Of course. This means a lot to you and your father, so I want to help."

"Okay then," Harmony agreed.

Harmony walked off to the tack room trying to figure out why Goliath was suddenly being so nice. When she got to the tack room she decided to get Spring from the field as the other horses had already done some work that morning.

Harmony took Spring back to the stable-yard where she found Goliath hard at work. After getting Spring ready, the two of them made their way round to the sand school. She waited until they were inside before mounting up. She warmed the horse up first before the real work began.

As Harmony rode Spring around the school she started to consider using Spring for the try-outs. Even though it had been a good workout on Spring, Harmony decided to stick with her first choice, Blizzard. She dismounted from Spring before heading back to the stable-yard to see how Goliath was getting on. When she got back he still had a couple of stables to do.

"How was your workout?" Goliath asked from one of the stables.

"It was good although I think there is still room for improvement," Harmony replied.

After untacking Spring, she took him to the field. She took the tack to the tack room then went around to the hay barn. Harmony still thought Goliath's behaviour seemed a little odd, consequently she decided to avoid him for a while.

After the way he had reacted when Freedom told him she would be taking Harmony to Elvesbridge it amazed her that he thought she would forgive him so easily. Harmony had not spoken to Freedom since the incident and she had no plans to anytime soon. Harmony was busy filling hay-nets when Rhoda joined her in the barn.

"Did I just see Goliath mucking out stables?" Rhoda asked.

"Yes. He came to see Father yesterday to see how I was doing," Harmony replied, slightly annoyed with Goliath.

She did not want her cousin to know that she might have feelings for him, she found it hard to believe herself.

Rhoda started helping Harmony fill the haynets. "What is going on with you and Goliath?" she asked suspiciously.

"Nothing is going on," Harmony replied innocently.

"Do you want there to be something going on between you and Goliath?" Rhoda asked inquisitively.

"Of course not. I am in love with Damien," Harmony said.

"Are you trying to convince me or yourself of that?" Rhoda asked, sensing confusion in her cousin's voice.

Once all the hay-nets were filled, Harmony knew she had to go back to the stable-yard where Goliath happened to be. As soon as she got back to the stable-yard, Harmony went straight to Tyson's stable to put the hay-net up, hoping not to be seen. While she was in the stable, Goliath came back with the water buckets.

"Thank you for helping me clean the stables," Harmony told him.

"What are friends for?" Goliath told her as he walked away.

Harmony quickly looked towards the stable door, completely caught off guard by what Goliath had said. She walked out of the stable hoping to find Goliath, only to see Rhoda stood in the yard. "Have you seen Goliath?" she asked.

"He just left," Rhoda said.

Harmony was just about to take the next hay-net into the next stable when her cousin stopped her.

"Why, did you need him for something?" Rhoda asked.

"No, it does not matter," Harmony replied. She walked into the next stable thinking about what Goliath had said when she thanked him for helping her.

The two girls finished off at the stable-yard before Rhoda went home.

CHAPTER FIFTEEN

Harmony went back to the cottage to start cooking the tea for when her father and brother returned home from work. She prepared all the vegetables and made a fresh loaf of bread to go with the dinner. Once all the preparation had been done she went upstairs to get washed and changed.

When Harmony came back downstairs she was wearing one of her new dresses. She went out to the kitchen to finish off the bread so that she could put it in the oven to bake. As it was quite cold outside she had decided to do lamb chops and gravy.

While everything was cooking, Harmony laid the table. She had just returned to the worktop to put the potatoes in a bowl when her father and brother entered through the backdoor.

"Something smells good," Raphael complimented her as he entered the room.

The two of them washed their hands before sitting at the table waiting for Harmony to bring the rest of the food. Once everything had been placed on the table she joined her father and brother.

After tea, Maurice and Raphael left the cottage which left Harmony to clean the kitchen. In a way she was glad to be kept busy as it meant she was not thinking about a certain person.

Once the kitchen had been cleaned, Harmony decided to go to her bedroom to read a book. She entered the bedroom lighting the candle on her bedside table to give her some light to see her book. Before she started reading, Harmony got changed ready for bed.

Harmony read her book until she heard her father come up to bed and then she put it down. She blew out the candle on her bedside table before snuggling under the duvet.

That night Harmony dreamed of her mother. She dreamed of when her mother became a patrol rider. She looked really pleased to have been chosen. She also saw the moment her mother got paired with Pride. He looked like Blizzard, the only difference between them was Pride was a stubborn horse. The main thing Harmony learned from her dream was that her mother never gave up, which gave Harmony even more determination to be chosen.

Although Harmony had planned to get up early in the morning, she woke up later than intended. Raphael ended up shaking his sister trying to wake her. After a while Harmony decided to give in and wake up.

"Come on, Harmony, we have got a lot of work to do," Raphael informed her.

Harmony rolled over to look at her brother. "I am coming. Can you let me get Blizzard ready?" she asked.

"Of course," Raphael answered, surprised that she had felt the need to ask. He walked out of the room to allow his sister to get ready.

Harmony reluctantly got out of bed and got dressed. All the time Harmony was getting ready she could not stop thinking about her dream. When she was ready she went downstairs for a quick breakfast, not wanting to waste another minute. "Good morning," Harmony greeted everyone.

"Good morning," the others replied, surprised to see Harmony so perky.

Harmony sat next to her brother at the table to eat her toast. She quickly ate her breakfast not wanting to waste any more time. After finishing her breakfast Harmony had a thought. She looked up at her brother. "Are the horses out in the field?" she asked.

Raphael looked at his sister. "Yes they are. I put them in the bottom half of the field this morning."

"That is good, hopefully they have used up some energy galloping around the field."

Maurice walked into the kitchen. "We had better get started. We have still got a lot of work to do."

Everyone got up from the table and put their boots on before heading to the stable-yard. When everyone arrived at the stables, Raphael went to grab the head-collars. The rest of them walked to the field to wait for him.

"Harmony, how come you decided not to ride Tyson at the try-outs?" Amos asked.

"He will not behave if he ends up between two horses. He has to be on the end of a row and I cannot guarantee that at the try-outs," she said.

When Raphael arrived, he handed out the head-collars while his father opened the gate. Tyson was the closest to the gate making it easy for Raphael to catch him. He then stood smiling, amused at the sight of his family walking across the field to find their horses.

Once all the horses had been caught they walked back to the stable-yard together. The horses were tied up outside their stables ready to be groomed. One at a time Harmony and the others went to the tack room to fetch the grooming kits.

Raphael looked up as Harmony returned with Blizzard's grooming kit as well as a couple of bottles. "What are those bottles for?" he asked.

"One of the bottles is to make his mane and tail easier to brush. The other is to try and bring out some of the shine in his coat," Harmony replied.

Raphael went back to grooming Tyson. He had a feeling his sister was going to be the last one ready.

The boys had just finished getting their horses ready when Harmony went to the tack room to fetch Blizzard's tack. She returned to the yard, still not hurrying even though her family were stood waiting. After what seemed like hours, Harmony finished tacking up Blizzard.

After making sure everything was perfect she went with the others to fetch their hats from the tack room. Before mounting onto their horses they listened to Maurice's plan.

"I thought today we would take Blizzard on a long ride all over the countryside. It will hopefully get him used to the different surroundings. We can then try him at different paces," Maurice informed them.

Everyone agreed with Maurice's plan, so they set off on their ride through the countryside. The lane from the stables was not big enough for them to ride side-by-side so they had to ride in pairs. At the end of the lane it opened on to a nice wide track which allowed them to ride alongside each other.

As the horses were well behaved they decided to make the ride more fun by having a race when the track turned soft. Harmony was enjoying being out on a ride with her family, especially her father.

At the end of the track, a road appeared that they had to cross. As they approached the road Blizzard started tensing up; he was not known for his bravery when it came to roads.

"How is Blizzard doing?" Maurice asked.

"He is tensing up a bit," Harmony said.

To everyone's surprise, Blizzard crossed the road without any trouble. Harmony patted her horse for crossing the road. They trotted along the lane hoping Blizzard would forget about the road. Little did they know he decided he had had enough training for one day.

As everyone approached a corner, Blizzard decided to bolt around it. Luckily Harmony managed to stop him just after the corner. Blizzard was not happy about being stopped and he would no longer behave for Harmony. The group walked along the next part of the lane to give Harmony a chance to gain control of Blizzard again. They were all happily riding along when they started to approach another road.

"Do you think Blizzard is ready to go along a road yet?" Maurice asked.

"I should think it would be okay. He seems to have calmed down," Harmony replied.

As they got nearer the road Blizzard started to tense up again. Everyone stopped at the end of the lane ready to ride on to the road. As Harmony asked Blizzard to walk forward, he refused and started to go backwards.

Raphael and Amos rode on to the road to make sure no one was coming, to give Harmony a chance to get on the road. After a few attempts there was only one option left. Amos and Raphael got off the road while Harmony rode back along the track away from the road. Once she had turned Blizzard around to face the right way, Raphael and Amos stood their horses on the road to check no one was coming along it.

Harmony cantered Blizzard along the track towards the road. As she got to the end of the track she slowed him to a trot. Not having time to think about what he was going to do, Blizzard trotted straight on to the road with little trouble.

To make things easier they decided to trot all the way along. Blizzard still hated being on the road so he tried to race the other horses. Harmony spent most of her time fighting him trying to hold him back.

After turning a few more corners, they were close to the boundary line where Harmony used to meet up with Damien. As they got closer, Harmony noticed a group of humans stood talking. They rode past the group causing one of them to look up.

"Harmony," the person called out to her.

She ignored them knowing her father would not be happy if she spoke to them.

"Harmony," the person called again.

This time Harmony looked up to see Damien looking at her. She rode over to him causing the rest of her family to stop.

"What is she doing?" Maurice asked.

"She is going to talk to Damien," Raphael answered.

When Harmony got to Damien she leaned down to give him a hug before sitting back up to say hello to the rest of her friends.

"I cannot stop for long, I have got an important try-out coming up. I have got to get in as much practice as possible."

"A try-out for what?" Damien asked.

"It is for a job," Harmony said.

"Harmony," Raphael called.

Harmony looked at her brother before looking at her friends. "I had better go, my family are getting impatient," Harmony told them. She said goodbye to her friends before leaning down to hug Damien again.

When Harmony returned to her family, she waved to her friends before leaving with her family. She could tell her father was not happy that she had gone over to her friends which Harmony had expected. She knew her family would never truly understand how much she missed her human life.

Maurice and Raphael were ignoring Harmony, leaving Amos to talk to her. "I know it is hard for you, Harmony, but you just have to put that life behind you now," he insisted. He was trying to be sympathetic towards her.

"I know I do, it just does not make it any easier. Let us leave it at that," Harmony told him, trying not to get angry that she was receiving another lecture.

By this point the boys could tell Harmony was annoyed. They decided to give her some space, so they dropped back a bit.

"What do you think she is upset about now?" Raphael asked.

"Let us just try to get through the rest of this ride without any more arguing," Maurice replied.

They managed to finish the ride without any more problems. When they got back to the yard everyone stopped their horses and dismounted.

"Can you two take care of the horses? I would like to talk to Harmony alone in the cottage," Maurice said.

"Okay," the boys replied.

Harmony followed her father through the back garden to the cottage. On the way to the cottage she knew that this talk would not end well for her.

CHAPTER SIXTEEN

At the stable-yard the boys were seeing to the horses.

"I would not want to be in her shoes right now," Amos admitted jokingly.

"I would not want to be in her shoes either," Raphael laughed too.

The boys put the horses in their stables before making their way back to the cottage. Raphael quietly opened the backdoor expecting to find his father and sister in the kitchen. As he looked into the room he was surprised to find it empty. He looked at Amos, confused. The cottage was quiet which made the boys think Maurice had taken Harmony to her bedroom where they would not be disturbed.

Just as they were about to walk into the hallway they heard raised voices coming from the living room. Amos led the way into the hallway to discover the living room door had been closed.

"He must have known we would be back before he finished," Raphael whispered.

"Well, by the sound of things, everything is going fine," Amos whispered.

Little did the two of them know events were about to take a bad turn.

"I THOUGHT YOU HAD CHANGED BUT I GUESS I WAS BEING DELUSIONAL TO THINK THAT YOU WOULD EVER BE A GOOD FATHER TO ME!" Harmony shouted.

Maurice looked up at his daughter. "I AM TRYING MY HARDEST... IT'S JUST, I NEVER WANTED A DAUGHTER!" Maurice shouted back angrily.

Harmony walked over to the door. "Fine. As of now you no longer have a daughter. You can also forget about me going to the try-outs. I am going back to the humans where I felt happy," she informed him.

"Fine!" Maurice shouted and then turned away from his daughter.

Harmony ran out of the living room and straight up to her bedroom.

Bewildered, the two boys looked at one another and then Raphael stepped into the living room. "What was all that about?" Raphael asked.

"We were just talking," Maurice answered innocently.

Raphael knew that that was not the case as he had been listening in the hallway with Amos. "Well I should know soon as Amos has gone to talk to her," Raphael informed him. He did not want to let his father know he had been listening at the door.

While Raphael had been talking to Maurice, Amos had made his way up the stairs to Harmony's bedroom. He knocked on the door and then waited to be invited in.

"GO AWAY!" Harmony shouted.

Amos could hear the sadness in her voice. "Come on, Harmony. I just want to talk to you."

"GO AWAY!"

"You know I am nothing like your father. I just want to know what he said to you. From where I was standing it sounded like he was completely out of line," Amos said, hoping to convince Harmony to talk to him.

The bedroom door opened slowly. Harmony stood in the doorway looking at the floor avoiding eye contact with her cousin. From what he could see she was still very upset at what her father had said.

"Was it really that unexpected?" Amos asked.

Harmony snapped her head up to look at her cousin. "Yes, it was. I cannot believe he could say that to me." Harmony was unable to hide her anger and disgust.

"Your brother and I heard what he said. We heard him say that he never wanted a daughter," Amos said calmly.

Harmony walked across her room to the window, then Amos followed her shutting the door behind him. Harmony looked at him as if to say, 'do not try to talk me into giving Father another chance.' He took hold of her hand before he carried on talking. "If what your father said is true, now is your chance to prove to him that a daughter is just as good as a son. You should go to the try-outs and make him proud as well as your mother."

Harmony looked out of her window trying to decide whether to go to the try-outs or not. "I will give it a try, but this is the last chance I am giving him," she sighed.

Pleased with what he had achieved, Amos walked towards the bedroom door. Just before leaving the room he turned back to Harmony. "I will see you tomorrow. We are going to have a lot to do."

"See you tomorrow," Harmony replied.

Amos left the room, shutting the door behind him. He went downstairs to go and talk to Raphael. He found his cousin sat at the kitchen table. Raphael looked up when he heard Amos walk in to the kitchen. "How is she?" he asked.

"She needs a break," Amos replied.

"I was planning on taking her out tomorrow. It would be even better if you and Rhoda came with us," Raphael said.

"Rhoda and I will come, but do not forget that Harmony has got to do all her final preparations for the try-outs tomorrow afternoon," Amos reminded him.

"I know, I have allowed for that," Raphael informed him.

"Okay, I will see you in a little while," Amos told him before leaving.

"See you in a little while," Raphael said as he got up from the table. He left the kitchen to go and tell his sister about the trip he had planned for the next day.

When Raphael got to his sister's bedroom, he knocked on the door. "Harmony, can I talk to you for a moment?"

Harmony opened her door before standing aside. "Sure," she said.

Raphael walked into the room before turning to face his sister. "Tomorrow I am taking you somewhere and Rhoda and Amos are coming with us."

"Where are we going?" Harmony asked.

"I am not going to tell you. All I am going to tell you is that we will need your car."

"Why will we need my car?" Harmony asked curiously.

"I cannot say. I will bring you some tea up so that you do not have to see Father," Raphael replied.

"Thank you," Harmony said seeming happier than she had done earlier.

Raphael left the room, leaving his sister to think about where he might be taking her. He went downstairs to the kitchen as he would be cooking the tea instead of Harmony. With no women in the house, as soon as he was old enough Raphael had to learn how to cook for his father.

While Raphael was cooking, Amos entered the kitchen. "Is Harmony joining us for tea tonight?" he asked.

"No, I told her I would take her tea up to her."

"We will need her to come down as we need to come up with a plan of action for tomorrow afternoon," Amos told him.

The two boys were stood in the kitchen when Maurice entered. "Where is she?" he asked.

Raphael looked at his father. "Harmony is in her room."

"She needs to be down here. There is a lot we still need to do tomorrow," Maurice said as he took a seat at the head of the table.

"I will ask her to come down if you promise to try to get along with her," Raphael informed him.

"If it gets tomorrow's plans sorted out," Maurice said reluctantly.

"Amos, would you mind getting Harmony for me," Raphael said.

Amos left the room to fetch his cousin for tea. He made his way to Harmony's bedroom, unsure of whether she would agree to come down or not. He knocked on the door and waited. Harmony opened the door expecting to see her brother stood there with a plate of food.

"Raphael and I need you to come downstairs to eat as we need to discuss plans for tomorrow," Amos informed her.

"Do I have to?" Harmony asked.

"I am afraid so," Amos said.

Harmony left her room following her cousin down the stairs. As the two of them entered the kitchen, Raphael was just putting the plates on the table. Amos walked over joining Raphael and Maurice. "Let us just eat our tea then we can discuss what we are going to do tomorrow," he suggested.

Harmony walked over to the table and picked up her plate. "If he is sitting at the table then I am not," she snapped, and then started to walk away from the table.

"Sit down, Harmony. I have told Father that he has got to make an effort to get along with you, and as a result, you have to make an effort as well," Raphael demanded.

Harmony reluctantly sat back down at the table. She ate her tea without even looking at her father as if he was not there. While they ate, nobody spoke which made Raphael happy as it was one time he did not have to play peacemaker between his father and sister. It was not until everyone had finished eating that the conversation began.

"Now that we have finished eating we need to discuss plans for tomorrow," Amos told them.

"Well, tomorrow morning Rhoda, Amos and I are taking Harmony out giving us tomorrow afternoon to get things ready," Raphael informed them.

Amos and Raphael looked at Harmony waiting to be told what needed doing to be ready for the try-outs.

"I cannot give you jobs to do until I have been down to the stable-yard to see what needs doing," she told them.

"When will you do that?" Raphael asked, starting to lose his patience with his sister.

"Once we have finished in here."

"Okay. Amos and I will do the washing and drying up if you go down to the stable-yard now, to see what needs doing," Raphael told her.

Maurice was going to say something about his son doing the clearing up, but Raphael looked at him telling him not to. With nothing else to do, Maurice got up from the table and retired to his study.

Harmony got up and headed to the boot room to wrap up warm, before heading out into the cold winter air.

At the stable-yard she made her way over to the tack room to pick up Blizzard's head collar and a torch. As it was getting darker by the minute she needed the torchlight to see the horses in the field.

When Harmony spotted Blizzard, she walked over to him slipping his head collar on his head. While she was facing the horse, she noticed him holding one of his legs off the ground. Harmony had a quick look at the leg and noticed a cut running down the side of it. Not liking the look of the cut, she decided to get him back to his stable. The journey was slow and painful as Blizzard struggled to put wait on his injured leg. When they arrived at the stable-yard Harmony decided to have another look at the cut now the light was better. After looking at it again she hated to admit it, but it looked a lot worse.

At the cottage, Amos had gone home and Raphael was getting ready to go and find his sister at the stables. Just like Harmony had done before, he was wrapping up as warm as possible.

As Raphael approached the stables, he was confused when he spotted Harmony stood with Blizzard on the yard. He was about to ask why when he noticed the horse holding his leg off the floor, he then spotted the cut down his leg. Raphael looked at Harmony. "Unfortunately, being elves we just have to stable them and hope it heals, as well as washing the cut regularly to keep it clean," he explained.

Harmony looked like she was close to tears. Raphael decided to find out what had happened before his sister got too upset to talk. "What happened?" he asked.

"I do not know. I found him in the field with the cut on his leg," Harmony answered.

"Put him in his stable then we will put the rest of the horses to bed," Raphael told her.

Harmony walked Blizzard to his stable while Raphael started putting the other horses into their stables. After closing the stable door, Harmony grabbed Tyson's head collar.

"What are you doing?" Raphael asked.

"I am going to get Tyson in from the field before washing the cut on Blizzard's leg."

Raphael knew that he would not be able to stop his sister so he just let her get on with it. As it was cold, all the horses had to have their blankets put on. Harmony finished off putting Tyson in his stable before walking to Blizzard's stable.

Raphael walked over to his sister after he had put the final horse in its stable. Harmony looked up at her brother. "You can go back to the cottage if you like. I am just going to use the hosepipe to clean Blizzard's leg. I get the feeling he is not going to like it one bit," she told him.

"That is okay. I will stay and watch just in case you need any help," he said.

Harmony took Blizzard from his stable over to the yard tap. She washed the cut which, as she predicted, Blizzard did not like. When she had finished, Harmony put Blizzard back in his stable. She patted his neck before saying goodnight to him. As soon as they were finished at the stables, Harmony walked with Raphael back to the cottage.

After unwrapping out of their winter wear in the boot room, the two of them walked towards the living room. Raphael entered the room, but Harmony stopped in the doorway. Raphael stopped before turning to look at his sister.

"I am going to bed," Harmony informed him.

"Okay, see you in the morning," Raphael said.

After saying goodnight to one another, the two of them went to bed.

CHAPTER SEVENTEEN

The next morning Harmony woke up to a crisp sunny morning. She got out of bed to get her clothes for the day. For the morning outing Harmony decided to wear her human clothing hoping the reason they needed her car was to visit where she lived with the humans. Harmony knew she should not get her hopes up but she could not think what else they would need her car for.

After choosing her morning outfit Harmony got out her stable clothes ready for an afternoon of hard work. She happily changed into her human clothes liking how comfortable they were as well as how they looked. She checked her outfit in the mirror before leaving her bedroom.

On her way to the bathroom she walked past her brother's bedroom, which to her surprise he had already left. Wanting to get going as soon as possible Harmony had a quick wash before rushing back to her bedroom to grab her bag. She looked around her room to make sure she had everything before running down the stairs for breakfast.

Harmony entered the kitchen out of breath to find her brother already sat at the kitchen table eating his breakfast. She joined her brother and made herself a bowl of cereal which she ate quickly. After she had finished eating, she was desperate to know what her brother had planned. "What is the plan this morning?" Harmony asked looking up at her brother.

Raphael put his spoon down on the table then looked up at his sister. "I will drive us to Yew Tree Cottage to pick up Amos and Rhoda. You will then drive all of us to Pebble Cove to show us what humans do for fun," Raphael answered.

Harmony started drinking her drink as fast as she could, at times almost choking on it.

"Maybe I should have waited until after you had finished your drink," Raphael said jokingly. He got up from his chair to clear away his breakfast things.

Once everything had been put away Harmony grabbed her bag causing her brother to smile as he knew how eager she was to leave.

"Are you ready?" Raphael asked.

"Absolutely," she replied sounding extremely happy.

On the way out of the cottage Harmony gave her car keys to Raphael, so he could drive to pick Amos and Rhoda, up as Harmony couldn't remember the way. He unlocked the car allowing them to get in. Harmony climbed in the front next to her brother. "Are you sure you want to do this?" she asked.

"Unlike Father, I am willing to give the humans a chance. Especially if it means you being happier," Raphael answered truthfully. He started the car to begin the short drive to Yew Tree Cottage.

On the journey Harmony had a thought. "What about Amos and Rhoda?" she asked.

"They feel the same way I do," Raphael reassured her.

After about ten minutes Raphael pulled on to a gravel drive. As they pulled on to the drive they passed by a wooden five-bar gate with a wooden sign on it saying 'Yew Tree Cottage'. The flint and brick cottage sat under a tiled roof surrounded by yew trees creating a nice shady hideaway.

Harmony and Raphael got out of the car to go and knock on the door. As they walked up to the front door Raphael handed his sister the car keys. "You will be the one needing those," he told her.

When they got to the oak wood door Raphael knocked a couple of times using the dormouse-shaped doorknocker. The two of them took a step back while they waited for the door to be opened. They did not have to wait long before Rhoda answered: "Good morning," she greeted them when she saw Raphael and Harmony stood in front of her.

"Good morning," Harmony and Raphael replied to their cousin.

Rhoda turned to look into the cottage. "Amos," she called.

He came out of the living room to see who was at the door. "Good morning," he said.

"Good morning," Harmony and Raphael replied.

"Are you ready to go?" Raphael asked.

"Yes, we are," Rhoda replied.

Rhoda and Amos followed Raphael and Harmony out of the cottage shutting the door behind them. The four of them walked across the drive to Harmony's car. Raphael got in the back with Amos while the two girls occupied the front seats.

"Where are we going?" Amos asked.

"We are going to a place called Pebble Cove. It is near where I used to live," Harmony said.

"Do you think you will see your friends?" Amos asked.

"I hope so. I have really missed them since I moved to Lilyleigh," Harmony said.

Harmony drove through Lilyleigh heading towards the boundary line she had crossed many times on Tyson. After crossing the bridge over the water, they approached their destination which made Harmony the happiest she had felt in a long time. She drove along the seafront looking for a parking space. It did not take her long to find a space close to the beach as the cold weather made it quieter. Harmony parked the car then turned to the others. "I will not be a minute, I just need to pay for parking," she informed them.

Amos, Rhoda and Raphael got out of the car while Harmony was gone.

"How come you brought your sister here?" Rhoda asked. "Your father will go mad if he finds out."

Raphael looked at her. "Will you relax. Harmony has been working hard getting ready for try-outs, hence I wanted her to do something that would make her happy and that she would enjoy," he replied.

"She was just coming round to the elves' way of living, finding out who she really is. Now she will be unsure again," Rhoda told him.

Raphael was just going to speak when Harmony arrived back at the car. She put the ticket on display in the front of the car before walking over to the other three. "I thought we could go for a walk along the beach first before getting a drink from the café to warm up," she informed them.

"If that is what you want to do," Raphael said.

Harmony locked the car then they made their way on to the beach. As soon as they stepped on the sand, Harmony stopped. Raphael also stopped to look at his sister who was now bent down. "What are you doing?" he asked.

"I am taking my shoes off to feel the sand between my toes."

Raphael took his shoes off causing Rhoda and Amos to stop. They looked at each other questioningly before they decided to do the same. Everyone picked up their shoes before making their way towards the sea. As it was a cold day they decided not to get their feet wet.

Harmony and Raphael stopped while Rhoda and Amos went for a walk along the sea edge. Raphael was stood looking out to sea, so Harmony decided to watch him. "What are you thinking about?" she asked.

"I am just trying to understand why you enjoy being with humans. I just cannot see it," Raphael said.

Harmony started looking out to sea, just as the answer to her brother's question came into view. "Damien," she said.

Raphael watched as his sister ran to him. "I guess that answers that one," he whispered to himself. He looked away when Harmony started cuddling Damien.

While Raphael was looking away from Harmony, Rhoda and Amos returned to join him.

"Where is Harmony?" Amos asked.

"She is with Damien," Raphael said disapprovingly.

Harmony stepped away from Damien before walking back to where she had been stood with her brother.

Damien followed cautiously behind her. He clearly had not forgotten his last encounter with her brother.

"Hello, Raphael. Hello, Amos," Damien greeted them politely.

Raphael turned to look at the human who had spoken to him. "Hello," he replied, trying to sound just as polite.

"Hello, Damien," Amos replied.

"Hello, Damien. I am Harmony's cousin Rhoda. I see you already know my brother Amos."

"Hello," Damien replied, not quite sure what to make of Rhoda yet. He relaxed slightly, glad that no one had tried to attack him. He stood next to Harmony, pleased that he was getting to spend some time with her.

"Damien, would you like to go for a walk?" Raphael asked.

Damien looked at Harmony wondering whether he should or not. Harmony nodded her head slightly in encouragement. Damien smiled at her before looking at Raphael again. "Sure," he replied.

Raphael walked away from the group, so Damien walked with him. Harmony watched nervously as the two of them walked further away from them. "What do you think Raphael wanted to talk to him about?" she asked.

"I do not know but I am sure it will be fine," Rhoda said, and then walked over to Harmony putting a comforting arm around her shoulders.

By now Raphael and Damien had reached the water's edge. Raphael stopped then began looking out to sea, which made Damien stop next to him. Damien stood looking out to sea, nervous of the topic of conversation Raphael had in store for him. He waited in silence for a minute or two before Raphael decided to start talking to him.

"You really like my sister don't you," Raphael said.

Damien looked at the elf surprised he did just want to talk. He was also surprised by the way the elf spoke; to him it sounded like a well-spoken character from a classic novel. It took him a moment to take everything in before he could find his voice again. "Yes, I do. I always knew she was the girl for me… ever since I first met her."

"So, you have known my sister for a long time," Raphael said.

"We started off as friends when we were young in school. Then as the years went by, we became closer until we decided that we should be together," Damien explained.

Raphael stood for a minute, deciding whether he was going to be honest with the human. In the end he decided he liked Damien enough to tell him the truth. "I know my sister likes you very much too. When she is at home she seems down, like a part of her is missing. Today when she saw you it was like a part of the old Harmony returned. She had a sparkle in her eyes that I have not seen for years," Raphael told him. Against his better judgement he was starting to like this human.

Raphael had found out what he wanted to know so the boys made their way up the beach to the group. As the two of them approached, Harmony was pleased to see that both the boys looked happy. When Raphael and Damien arrived back at the group, Harmony looked at Damien. "How about we go to Bandit Cove?" she asked.

"That sounds good. There are more things to do," Damien replied.

The group walked together back to the car. Raphael climbed in the back with Rhoda and Amos allowed Damien to sit in the front with Harmony.

"When we get there, we can grab a drink at the café to warm up," Damien suggested.

At Bandit Cove, Harmony parked the car in the car park. While Damien went to pay for parking, everyone got out of the car. Damien came back with the ticket and put it on display in the front of the car. "Where are we going to first?" he asked.

Harmony locked the car and put the keys in her little bag. "I think we should go to the café first as I am starting to get a little thirsty," she said.

Damien looked at the other elves. "Is that okay?"

"Yes, it is fine," the others replied.

The five of them walked around the corner to the café. Damien opened the door then stood holding it open for everyone to enter. Harmony walked in first, closely followed by the rest of her family. Damien followed them, watching Harmony's relatives as they looked at the café. "What do you want to drink?" he asked.

"We will have a cup of tea," Raphael answered.

"What about you, Harmony?" Damien asked, wondering if she would stick with her brother's choice or have her favourite.

Harmony looked at her brother while she thought about her choices. In the end she could not resist getting her favourite drink while she had the chance. "I will have a hot chocolate please," she said.

"Okay, you lot find a table while I get the drinks," Damien instructed.

Harmony found a table with her family by the window to sit at to admire the view. Harmony's family sat opposite, to let Damien sit next to her. Harmony sat watching Damien carry the drinks across the café on a tray, which would have been a regular occurrence for her.

Damien put the tray on the table before handing everyone their drinks. Once the tray was empty he took it back before sitting down next to Harmony. "How about after we finish these drinks we go for another walk?" Damien asked.

"I would love to see some more of the old places we used to hang out at," Harmony replied.

"Is this one of the places you used to hang out at?" Rhoda asked.

"I should think out of all the places this is where we used to spend the most amount of time," Damien said.

"Only because you boys would go out on your jet skis while all the girls were on the beach sunbathing," Harmony told him.

They all took a sip from their drinks which were still nice and hot before putting them back down on the table. As Harmony put her cup down she had a thought. "Is the rope swing we made in the woods still there?" she asked.

"Not anymore," Damien said.

"What happened to it?" Harmony asked.

"Brett broke it," Damien said.

Amos looked at Harmony. "Did you ever spend any time at home?" he asked.

"Not really. I had so many hobbies and friends that I was always out doing something," Harmony said.

Once everyone had finished their drinks they got up to leave. Damien led the way out of the café to the second beach of the day. As they reached the beach, Amos, Rhoda and Raphael dropped back slightly.

"When are you going home?" Damien asked.

"After this walk I expect," Harmony said.

Damien looked down. He had been hoping that he could have more time with Harmony. He walked along the beach holding hands with Harmony, feeling like the events of the last couple of years had never happened.

"I think we should be heading home now, Harmony," Raphael called to her.

"Okay," Harmony called back, sounding down about having to leave Damien again.

Harmony stepped toward Damien and the two of them started hugging. Without realising what they were doing they started kissing. Raphael turned away, still unable to handle the fact that his sister was deeply in love with a human. "I wish they would not do that," he told his cousins.

Amos could tell that Raphael was totally against Harmony and Damien. He then realised something else. "Is that why you want her to do the patrol rider try-outs?" he asked.

Raphael looked at Amos. "Of course it is. With any luck she will see an elf that catches her eye and she will forget all about Damien," he said, sounding confident with his plan. He looked over to where Harmony had been walking with Damien as she was walking towards them alone.

Once Harmony got back to the group they decided to leave. As they walked back along the beach, Harmony glanced over her shoulder. At that moment Raphael realised how much his sister missed Damien when she was at home. Nobody spoke, even when they got back to the car.

On the journey home Harmony turned to look at her brother. "Thank you for today. I had a really good time."

"What was the best part?" Rhoda asked.

"I would say it was getting to see Damien again."

"Speaking of Damien, you miss him when we are at home, do you not?" Raphael asked.

"I do miss him. I miss all my friends. It is a shame it is not going to change anything though," Harmony replied.

Raphael became quiet as he noticed the sudden change in his sister's feelings. They had gone from being happy and cheerful to unhappy. Not wanting to remind her of what she was leaving behind, he decided not to say anything else about their morning.

"What are we doing this afternoon?" Rhoda asked.

"We are getting ready for tomorrow," Raphael said.

The rest of the journey was silent as everyone tried to avoid the subject of Damien, which Raphael found very easy to do.

CHAPTER EIGHTEEN

Harmony pulled into the gravel drive before parking in front of the garage. They all climbed out of the car and headed into the cottage. When they walked through the front door they spotted Maurice sat in the living room in front of a roaring fire, looking through some paperwork.

"Hello, Father," Raphael greeted him.

"Hello, Raphael," Maurice returned.

Rhoda and Amos stepped forward and greeted their uncle.

Amos, Rhoda and Raphael looked at Harmony, so she stepped in to the room. "Hello, Father," she greeted him nervously.

"Hello, Harmony." Maurice once again returned the greeting. He put the paperwork down on the table next to him before looking at his daughter. "Are you ready for some hard work?" he asked.

"I guess so," Harmony replied.

"Who is going to do which job?" Amos asked.

"I think Rhoda and I will give Spring a bath. Father and Raphael can wash the horsebox, and Amos can get the inside of the horsebox ready," Harmony instructed.

Everyone seemed happy with their jobs so they all left the cottage heading for the stable-yard. Having had their instructions back at the cottage, everybody got straight to work hoping it would help them keep warm.

The male members of the family tackled cleaning the horsebox while Rhoda helped Harmony wash Spring. While they were rubbing the shampoo into Spring's coat Harmony could feel someone watching her. She turned to look towards the horsebox to find her father watching her. She smiled at him before turning her attention back to the horse.

"What are you smiling about?" Rhoda asked.

"The family working together, it is how I always wanted it to be," Harmony replied.

They took Spring back to his stable then Rhoda left to help her mother at home. Harmony made her way to the tack room to get Spring's saddle and bridle to clean in the boot room where it would be warmer.

Amos finished his jobs then walked over to Harmony. "Is there anything else you would like me to do?" he asked.

"If you could help my father and brother finish cleaning the horsebox, that will be all the outside jobs done. I will come down later to check on Spring."

While the boys worked on the horsebox, Harmony went to the tack room to fetch Spring's tack. Not wanting to work in the cold, she decided to take it all back to the cottage. Knowing her father would not be happy if she made a mess in the cottage, Harmony had to clean the tack in the boot room.

As Harmony was cleaning the tack it occurred to her how much effort she was putting into making everything perfect. It surprised her because it would mean she had chosen the elves over the humans. This idea scared her as she had not planned on choosing between them, instead she had still hoped to find the perfect balance between the two worlds. While she cleaned the tack, she continued to think about what becoming a patrol rider would mean.

Harmony was just putting Spring's bridle back together when Amos walked into the boot room. "Are you okay?" he asked.

"Yes, I am just thinking about tomorrow."

"What were you thinking about?"

"It just occurred to me that my life is now with the elves instead of the humans," she said.

"You make it sound like a bad thing," Amos said.

"I had hoped to keep my options open for longer," Harmony informed him.

Amos washed his hands while Harmony finished off cleaning the tack. After Harmony had finished the tack cleaning she had to take it back to the stable-yard.

"Would you like some help with that?" Amos asked.

"Yes please. You can take the saddle."

Amos picked up the saddle while Harmony grabbed the bridle with the martingale. The two of them made their way back to the stable-yard, carrying the tack that had just been cleaned.

"Where are we putting this?" Amos asked.

"It can go straight in the horsebox ready for the morning," Harmony said.

Amos opened the tack locker inside the horsebox before turning to Harmony. "Have you got much more to do?" he asked as he put the saddle on its rack.

Harmony hung up the bridle before turning to her cousin. "I want to make sure that everything I need is in the horsebox. I need to clean Blizzard's leg before I feed the other horses. The tea also needs heating up."

Amos could not believe how much his cousin still had to do. "How about your brother and I take care of Blizzard's leg as well as feeding the horses?" he asked.

"That would be really helpful, thank you," Harmony said and gave her cousin a hug before he left.

Harmony carried on checking through the horsebox making sure everything was as it should be, present and correct. By the time she had finished, Harmony had been through the horsebox at least three times. Once she felt absolutely certain everything was as it should be, she closed up the horsebox so she could head back to the cottage.

When Harmony entered the boot room she swapped her stable boots for her slippers. After changing her footwear she made her way upstairs to change out of her riding clothes into one of her dresses she wore for doing chores. Harmony felt relieved that her brother was putting the horses in for the night with the help of Amos as it meant she could focus on the dinner.

After changing her clothes, Harmony made her way down to the warmth of the kitchen where she started to warm up the stew Raphael had made the day before. She had just started cutting up the crusty loaf of bread when the boys walked in. She looked up at them to see they were dirty from being at the stables. "Go and get cleaned up, dinner will be about fifteen minutes," she told them.

The three of them left the kitchen to get cleaned up leaving Harmony to set the table ready for when they came back down. Harmony had started to put the stew in the bowls when Amos walked into the kitchen in clean clothes. "Are the other two on their way?" she asked.

"Yes, they should be here in a minute," Amos answered.

Harmony continued to fill the bowls with stew and Amos helped her carry them to the table. Harmony and Amos stood by the table waiting for Maurice and Raphael to come down. They stood waiting for a couple of minutes before the two boys appeared. After Maurice sat down, the rest of them took their seats.

"Let us eat," Maurice instructed.

As usual there was no talking whilst eating, which was how Maurice always had it. The boys were eating a lot faster than Harmony causing Raphael to keep looking at his sister. Harmony found it difficult to eat as she kept thinking about the patrol rider try-outs the next day.

Once everyone had finished eating, Raphael decided to find out how his sister was feeling about the try-outs. "Are you okay?" he asked.

"I am just feeling nervous about tomorrow," she said.

Now that everyone had finished, Maurice got up from the table before making his way into the lounge. As her father had left, Harmony started clearing the table so she could get on with the washing up.

"Amos and I can do that if you want," Raphael offered.

"No thank you. It is keeping me busy... helping me not to think about tomorrow," Harmony told him.

Raphael and Amos left the kitchen to join Maurice in the living room. When they entered the room, Maurice was sat in his armchair waiting for them. Raphael and Amos sat on the sofa, realising he had been waiting for them.

"How do you think Harmony feels about tomorrow?" Maurice asked.

"She seems so nervous, I actually think she cares about becoming a patrol rider," Raphael said.

"Why do you think that would be?" Amos asked.

"It would appear she has finally accepted that this is where she belongs," Raphael said.

The three of them were sat reading when Harmony appeared in the doorway after clearing away the dinner things. "I am going up to bed now. Goodnight," she said.

Amos and Raphael said goodnight, then Harmony started to walk away.

"Goodnight, Harmony," her father said unexpectedly.

"Goodnight, Father," Harmony returned. She left the room completely shocked that her father had said goodnight to her.

As soon as Harmony reached her bedroom she changed out of her dress into her chemise before climbing into bed. Not long after Harmony had gone up to bed Raphael went up, closely followed by Amos. Amos was sharing a room with Raphael as there was no space in the spare bedroom.

Before going to Raphael's room, Amos stopped outside Harmony's bedroom. He knocked quietly on the door before waiting to be invited in.

"Come in," Harmony called.

Amos opened the door and then entered the room. "Your brother and I were just wondering if we were still getting up at six tomorrow morning to help you?"

"I would prefer it if you did not. I would like to get Spring ready on my own."

"Okay, that's fine, we just wanted to make sure," Amos said, and then made his way to Raphael's room.

"What did she say?" Raphael asked.

"She wants to do it on her own," Amos said as he climbed into bed.

"I thought she would, because that is how Mother would have done it," Raphael told him.

"At least we will have an extra hour in bed," Amos said gladly.

CHAPTER NINETEEN

The next morning Harmony woke up before dawn. She got out of bed to get dressed. Not wanting to get her try-out clothes dirty she put on her everyday stable clothes.

After she had got dressed Harmony quietly made her way through the cottage to the backdoor. She put her wellington boots on before leaving for the stables. It was so early it was quite dark outside as well as cold. As there were no lights on, Harmony decided to use a torch until she could put the lights on down at the stables.

When Harmony got to the stables Spring was at his stable door waiting for her. As a morning treat she gave him a carrot to make up for getting him out of his stable so early. While Spring was eating his carrot Harmony went to the stable next door to see Blizzard. She held out her hand with a carrot for him. He slowly limped over to her to get the carrot. As Blizzard took the carrot she stroked his head and neck.

When Blizzard returned to the back of his stable Harmony turned her attention to Spring. Once he was ready for the journey ahead she did not want Spring to roll in his stable so she left him tied up outside.

Harmony went back to the cottage to grab some breakfast and to see if the boys were awake. When she entered the cottage the boys were in the kitchen. She took her coat and boots off before joining them in the warmth.

"Where did you put Spring?" Maurice asked.

"I tied him up outside his stable," she said. She made herself some toast then joined the others at the kitchen table. "Once we have eaten breakfast we will load the rest of the equipment into the horsebox. We will then load Spring so that we can get going."

They all nodded, agreeing with the suggestion. After everyone had finished breakfast they got going with the plan Harmony had suggested. As it was so cold outside they all had their warm winter clothing on to try to keep warm.

The boys loaded the equipment into the horsebox while Harmony loaded Spring. Now that everything had been placed in the horsebox they drove off to the try-outs. As Harmony was feeling nervous, no one spoke throughout the entire journey.

When they arrived at the location of the try-outs there were lots of horseboxes as well as trailers. Maurice parked the horsebox then they all got out.

"Oh no," Harmony said alarmed.

"What is it?" Raphael asked, worried they had forgotten something important.

"They are letting people walk around to watch us groom our horses," Harmony said.

Maurice ignored his daughter's reaction. "Let us just get on with preparations and pretend they are not here," he said reassuringly.

Harmony looked at her father knowing he was right. "Okay then," she said reluctantly.

Amos helped Raphael slowly lower the ramp of the horsebox. Harmony walked up the ramp and untied Spring. She led him down the ramp before tying him to the side of the horsebox. "Can one of you take off his travel set please?" Harmony asked.

Raphael took off Spring's travel set. While he was doing that, Harmony got the grooming kit out of the horsebox. When she returned the three boys were stood doing nothing. "How about you three make yourselves useful? Go and have a look around at the other horses," she told them. By now she was starting to sound panicky.

The boys turned around and walked off into the crowd to let Harmony get on with things. Harmony had started grooming Spring when a voice called her name. She looked up just as Damien peeked over the top of Spring.

"What are you doing here?" Harmony asked, surprised to see him.

"I followed you back to your cottage before following you here."

Harmony carried on grooming Spring. "Why would you do that?"

Damien put his hand on Harmony's shoulder. "I had to see my girlfriend. I also need to talk to you about something important."

Harmony finished brushing Spring then she started plaiting his mane and tail. While she was doing so a young male elf walked over to them.

"He is a pretty horse. What is his name?" the elf asked.

"His name is Spring," Harmony said.

The young man looked up at Harmony and Damien. "I am so sorry, you must think I have no manners. What are your names?" he asked.

"My name is Harmony. This is my cousin Damien," Harmony replied.

The young man shook their hands. "It is nice to meet you. My name is Pixel."

"It is a pleasure to meet you, Pixel," Harmony said politely.

The two boys stood watching Harmony as she finished plaiting Spring. After she had done so, she sent Damien into the horsebox to get the horse's tack. Harmony stood waiting for him with Pixel. "Are you watching the try-outs?" she asked.

"I am, even more so now I know you are trying out," Pixel answered starting to flirt with her.

Harmony and Pixel were stood looking at each other, their eyes connecting, ignoring everything going on around them.

Damien was just about to step out of the horsebox when he spotted Maurice returning with Raphael and Amos. He stood hidden just inside the horsebox, wondering if Harmony knew her family were on their way back. As Damien watched, Harmony and Pixel slowly leaned towards each other. Before Damien could do anything, they were kissing.

When Raphael spotted his sister kissing the elf he suggested that the rest of them should walk around again.

"I agree. This could be the elf we have been waiting for, the one to make her happy," Amos agreed.

Even Maurice looked happy at the sight of his daughter with the elf. The three boys walked off to give Harmony and the elf more time alone. What the three boys did not know was that Harmony's human boyfriend Damien was stood inside the horsebox.

Damien walked down the steps carrying Spring's tack. Harmony stepped back from Pixel when she heard her boyfriend coming.

"Harmony, how could you do that to me? After all of the rules I have broken to be with you," Damien said angrily.

"I did not ask you to break the rules," Harmony told him.

"I know you didn't. I did it because I love you," he said in a much calmer tone.

"Damien, I told you ages ago that I would not be able to see you any more," she reminded him.

"Fine, if that's the way you want it to be, you will never see me again," Damien told her. He shoved Spring's tack into Harmony's arms before storming off.

"Damien, wait, I'm sorry," Harmony called after him.

Damien never stopped to look at her, instead he just carried on running.

"I am tired of trying to please everyone and prove myself as an elf. All it ever does is go wrong. I am trying my hardest to be an elf but it is losing me my human friends, which is not what I wanted to happen," Harmony explained to Pixel.

"I am guessing Damien was not who you said he was," Pixel stated.

"No, he was not," Harmony admitted. She gave Spring's saddle to Pixel to hold while she put the horse's bridle on.

While Harmony was gently checking the bridle had been fitted correctly, Pixel decided to find out what was going on. "Damien was not your cousin, was he?" he asked suspiciously.

Harmony knew she could not lie anymore. "No, he was not. He was my boyfriend."

Pixel carefully placed the saddle on the horse's back.

"Why did you not tell me?" he asked.

"My family do not approve, so they are hoping I find a boyfriend here." She was starting to wish Pixel had not brought the subject up.

"Why does your family not approve? He seems like a really nice person," Pixel said.

Harmony secured Spring's saddle by doing up the girth straps. "I know. He is not bad for a human," she said.

Pixel was stunned into silence.

Harmony waited for Pixel to say something. While she was waiting, she checked the horse's saddle had been placed correctly.

Time had moved along quicker than anyone had noticed. Harmony's family quickly went back to the horsebox to wish Harmony good luck for the try-outs. Pixel also wished Harmony good luck before kissing her on the cheek. Raphael gave her a leg up before leaving with the others to find their seats to watch the try-outs.

After the boys had left, Harmony felt very confused. She had enjoyed Pixel's kiss more than she should have. Knowing she did not have time to think about it at that moment she tightened Spring's girth ready to go.

"Here we go, Spring." Harmony sighed. She walked her horse over to the arena. When she got to the waiting area there were more horses there than she had expected.

CHAPTER TWENTY

By now the boys had managed to find their seats in the stand. They sat watching the girls try out to see what standard of riding Harmony was up against. There were five girls that tried out before Harmony, creating a mixed standard of riding. Up next it was Harmony's turn in front of the judges, which made the boys nervous.

Harmony quietly walked Spring into the arena. She stopped him in front of the judges awaiting her first instructions.

"Welcome, Harmony. Could you please do a circuit of the arena in walk? I would then like you to halt your horse in front of the judges," the judge instructed.

Harmony nodded towards the judge before she got Spring into a nice calm walk. After completing the circuit of the arena in walk, Harmony halted her horse where she started from in front of the judges. The judges made some notes before speaking to her again. "If you could do a circuit of the arena in trot followed by a circuit in canter?"

Harmony got Spring to do a few strides of walk before asking him to go in to a trot. While trotting around the arena, Spring started to get a bit lively, which made Harmony nervous. She hoped and prayed that he would wait until she asked for canter before he started cantering.

As the two of them approached the marker where they would start cantering, Harmony could feel Spring anticipating the next move. She could feel the horse getting quite tense so she asked him to start cantering a couple of strides earlier than she should have done. Spring calmed down as soon as he was cantering, allowing Harmony to relax as well.

As the two of them approached the judges, Harmony slowed her horse down ready to stop in front of them. After she had stopped her horse facing the judges, they all finished making notes about what they had seen.

"Okay, Harmony, that will be enough for now. We will let you know when we have made our decision," the head judge informed her.

"Thank you," Harmony replied politely. She rode Spring out of the arena hoping she had done enough. She also hoped Spring's excitement in trot did not ruin her chances.

After leaving the arena, Harmony decided to ride back to the horsebox to await the results. She dismounted from Spring before tying him to the horsebox. After seeing to her horse she sat on the steps of the horsebox thinking about how he tensed up before they started cantering, which he had never done before.

Not wanting to sit alone with her thoughts, Harmony got up off the steps before walking into the horsebox to get the bucket of water. She carried the bucket down the steps to the horse and put the bucket on the floor. She lifted the lid off the bucket allowing the horse to drink the water.

After Spring had finished having a drink, Harmony tied him back up to the horsebox. After making sure the horsebox was all shut up, Harmony untied Spring and then walked him over to the waiting area where all the other horses and riders were. Before joining the other riders Harmony mounted up. She had not been back in the waiting area long before all the riders were called into the main arena.

Everyone rode into the main arena where they stood their horses in a circle around the edge. The head judge walked in to the middle of the circle then looked at all the riders before she began speaking. "We have only ten riders moving on to the next round," she informed them.

All the riders looked at each other wondering who had got through. The riders looked back at the judge eager to know who had made it. The judge read out nine names, the ninth person to get through was a young lady named Trixie.

Harmony felt sure she had failed because her name had not been read out. She hated that all her practising on

Blizzard had gone so well and now she could have failed because the horse she wanted to use had been injured. Harmony watched nervously as the judge looked at her piece of paper once more before looking at the riders.

"The final rider going through to the second round is Harmony Redvers."

Harmony cuddled Spring's neck, overjoyed that she had made it through to the next round. While she was celebrating in the arena, her family were clapping and cheering for her. Harmony felt relieved that all her worrying had been for nothing.

The judge thanked the riders who had not got through for trying out. The riders who had not made it left the arena, allowing the riders who had got through to do a lap of honour around the arena.

When Harmony arrived back at the horsebox, Pixel was stood waiting for her. He held on to Spring's reins while she dismounted. Harmony gave Pixel a hug happy at the thought of being one step closer to being a patrol rider. While the two of them were hugging, Maurice arrived back at the horsebox with Raphael and Amos.

"I guess we had better sort out the horse," Maurice joked. He gently took the reins from Pixel's hand to be able to sort Spring out.

When Harmony finally stopped hugging Pixel she introduced him to her family. She pointed to each family member as she told him their names. "This is my cousin Amos, my older brother Raphael and my father Maurice."

Raphael looked at his sister. "What is his name?"

"This is Pixel."

Pixel looked at Harmony. "The young man I met earlier was your boyfriend Damien, is that correct?" he asked.

Harmony could not believe what she had just heard. She looked at Pixel completely annoyed with him. "I cannot believe you just said that."

The three boys were looking at Harmony, shocked by this news. Maurice walked over to his daughter trying to contain his anger. "Is it true what he just told us about Damien?" he asked still trying to fight his anger.

Harmony nodded knowing that the answer she really wanted to give would make her father angrier.

"Answer me properly when I ask you a question," Maurice exclaimed.

Harmony decided it was time to finally stand up to her father by answering back. "Yes, Damien was here. I am glad he was, as he is someone I miss a lot when he is not around."

Maurice slapped Harmony hard across the face. Harmony quickly placed her hand on her cheek, shocked by what her father had just done to her. She then watched as her father walked away from the horsebox, followed by Amos and Pixel.

As soon as Maurice and his followers were out of sight, Raphael turned his attention to his sister. "Are you okay?" he asked concerned.

"I am fine, I just want to get this over and done with. I knew I should never have given him another chance."

Raphael helped his sister mount on to Spring. "Good luck," he said.

"Thank you," she replied.

Raphael walked away to the stands to take his seat. He had just sat down when all the riders entered the arena, and from that moment he never took his eyes off his sister.

The head judge spoke to the riders from the judges' table. "If you split into two groups of five we will begin," she explained.

The riders quickly got into two groups of five eager to carry on with the next part of the try-outs.

"If the group nearest the gate leaves the arena, we will look at the group nearest to us first," the judge instructed.

The group nearest the gate left the arena, leaving the group Harmony was in to be tested first. The riders lined up their horses side by side in front of the judges' table. Harmony ended up in the middle of the row of horses, which Spring did not seem bothered by at all. She was just glad that she had not decided to bring Tyson to the try-outs.

The judge looked up from her papers. "Instead of riding around the edge of the arena you are going to be riding from one end to the other," she instructed.

Everyone rode to the end of the arena opposite the judges. They all turned their horses so that they were facing towards the judges' table.

"The first thing we are going to test is the stopping ability of the horses. I want you to canter towards us, one by one, instantly stopping in front of us," the judge instructed.

Some of the girls seemed very nervous about the task they had been set. The first girl who tried had to make a sudden detour as her horse was definitely not going to stop. The second girl's horse went from canter to trot to walk before stopping in front of the judges.

Next it was Harmony's turn. She kicked Spring into a canter. As Spring took off at a canter he decided to buck. Although she had not been expecting it, Harmony carried on as if nothing had happened. She was approaching the judges very quickly. The atmosphere in the arena was very tense. Just before getting to the judges, Harmony pulled hard on Spring's reins. The two of them managed to stop about an inch from the judges' table. Out of the five riders only two of them managed to stop in front of the judges.

The second task they were given had them line up next to each other against the bottom end of the arena opposite the judges. The task was to go from one end of the arena to the other in each of the paces whilst staying side by side.

After the tasks had finished, the group left the arena ready for the second group to enter. The second group then had to complete the same tasks as the first group of riders.

Outside the arena, Harmony was patting Spring and telling him what a good job he had done. While they were waiting to go back into the arena a young lady roughly the same age as Harmony rode over to her.

"Hello, my name is Trixie. This is my horse Cleopatra," the young lady informed her.

"Hello, Trixie, my name is Harmony, and this is my horse Spring."

The two of them sat looking at each other.

"I was so nervous about trying out. I think Cleopatra could sense my nerves," Trixie explained.

"I could not tell that you were nervous. You were better than me and Spring. I have never known him act like that," Harmony said. She had just finished speaking when they heard the judge's voice.

"Could all riders please return to the arena," the judge called.

All the riders rode back into the arena. The atmosphere became very tense as the final wave of nerves spread across the group. As there were less of them, the riders lined up side by side. Harmony stood Spring next to Trixie and Cleopatra.

"When I call your name, if you could walk forwards, as you will be our new patrol riders," the judge informed them.

All the girls sat nervously awaiting their fate. The judge collected together the papers of the girls who had made it.

"The first patrol rider is Trixie," the judge announced.

Trixie rode Cleopatra forward. As she rode forward the crowd were clapping along with the other riders. Trixie seemed very pleased to have become a patrol rider. She smiled as she looked around the arena at the crowd.

The judge read out three more names of which Harmony's was not one of them. The crowd continued clapping for the girls who had been chosen. Even though the riders were pleased for those who had made it, their nerves were at their highest as they knew there was only one spot left.

"Now it is time to hand out the role of head patrol rider. This honour is going to a rider who proved today she can handle anything that is thrown at her. I am pleased to announce that Harmony is head patrol rider," the judge announced cheerfully.

Harmony walked Spring forward to join the line of patrol riders. The crowd clapped for the final line up of new patrol riders. Raphael was cheering along with Amos. Maurice was sat next to Amos, reluctantly clapping for his daughter. Harmony looked up surprised by her father's reaction.

Once all the clapping had ceased the judge spoke to the five girls. "Could you please come to the table to pick up your uniforms? I would like Harmony at the back of the line," she instructed.

Each of the riders rode past the judges to collect their uniforms. When Harmony got to the table the judge did not give her the uniform straight away. Instead, the judge looked up at her. "I would like you to inform the other riders that your first duty is tomorrow morning," the judge instructed. She informed Harmony of her duties before finally giving her a uniform.

After receiving her uniform Harmony rode over to where the other girls had gathered. The girls looked up when they heard a horse approaching them. Harmony stopped Spring in front of the group. "Our first duty is tomorrow. We have got to escort our king and queen to their holiday home in time for Christmas. While she is staying there, we will also have to stay to patrol the boundary," she informed them.

The girls looked at each other wanting to see each other's reaction to the task. They all seemed comfortable with their first assignment.

"What time have we got to meet?" Trixie asked.

The group looked at their leader for the final instructions.

"We are to meet at the castle at eight o clock tomorrow morning," Harmony said.

"Thank you for letting us know," Trixie said gratefully.

"I will see you tomorrow morning bright and early," Harmony said, and then rode away from the girls back to the horsebox.

As Harmony approached the horsebox all the boys started clapping. Pixel walked over to her. He took hold of Spring's reins so that he could lead them in. When Spring stopped, Harmony dismounted and Raphael took Spring's reins from Pixel.

"Harmony, may I speak with you alone for a moment?" Pixel asked.

"Of course," and she followed Pixel away from her family.

Pixel stopped when they were far enough away. He turned to face Harmony who had stopped behind him. Pixel looked at the ground, nervous about what he was going to ask her. Harmony walked closer to Pixel and put her hand gently on his shoulder. He looked at her suddenly remembering he was not alone.

"I know we only met each other today but I really like you and I do not want to lose you to anyone else. So, Harmony, will you court me?" Pixel asked.

Harmony was surprised by Pixel's question. She thought for a moment about Damien but then she realised that her time with the humans had come to an end. "I would love to court you," she said.

The two of them kissed before walking back to the horsebox, hand in hand. As Harmony approached the horsebox with Pixel, the family noticed the two of them holding hands.

"Are you two courting now?" Amos asked.

Both Harmony and Pixel smiled. Harmony nodded to answer her cousin's question. She then looked at her father who managed to smile at the news.

"It is a shame that we are not allowed alcohol," Harmony moaned.

"I guess it is a night of drinking water as usual," Amos said, trying to sound happy about it.

While Harmony could see that her father was happy she took the opportunity to ask him if Pixel could join them to celebrate. "Father, would it be okay if Pixel came home with us?" she asked.

"Of course he can," Maurice answered.

The boys were putting the equipment into the horsebox while Pixel helped Harmony get Spring ready for travelling. Once everything had been packed away everyone squeezed into the horsebox.

CHAPTER TWENTY-ONE

On the way home everyone except Harmony was talking about the try-outs. Harmony had cuddled up to Pixel to think about how proud her mother would be that she had become head patrol rider.

"Father, do you think Blizzard's leg will be healed soon?" Harmony asked.

"I think it will be a few weeks before his leg will be healed. You will then only be able to lightly ride him, so no I do not think it will be healed soon," Maurice answered.

Pixel pulled Harmony closer to him and the conversation died down. When they arrived at the cottage they drove the horsebox straight to the stable-yard. Raphael parked the horsebox in its normal place not too far from the stables. After Amos had lowered the ramp Harmony unloaded Spring walking him straight to his stable.

"Once you have sorted out Spring, can you check on Blizzard," Raphael called out to Harmony.

After Harmony had settled Spring in his stable she went to check on Blizzard. As she looked in the stable, Harmony noticed it was empty. She looked at the ground and found a trail of blood leading away from the stable. She then realised that Blizzard had broken through the stable door as it was where the trail of blood began. Harmony ran back to the horsebox as fast as she could. "Get Spring's tack out of the lorry," Harmony instructed urgently.

The boys looked at her confused.

"NOW!" Harmony shouted at them.

"What is wrong?" Raphael asked as he started to walk towards his sister.

"Blizzard has gone. He must have made the cut on his leg worse by breaking through his stable door. There is blood everywhere," Harmony said frantically to make them realise how serious the situation was. She then started crying, fearing the worst for Blizzard.

"I will go with you to look for him," Raphael told her. He put his arm around his sister's shoulders before turning to look at Pixel. "Can you catch a horse?" he asked.

"Yes, I can," Pixel said matter-of-factly.

"Can you go and catch me one of those horses?" Raphael asked pointing at the bottom field.

Pixel grabbed a head collar then ran to the field catching the horse closest to him. He then ran back to the yard with Tyson in tow. When he arrived at the yard Raphael had already mounted onto Spring who had been tacked up while Pixel was in the field. Maurice stood next to Spring, holding Tyson's tack ready for when he got to the yard.

Harmony quickly put her horse's bridle on while her father tackled his saddle. Maurice tightened Tyson's girth before Amos gave Harmony a leg up. Once Harmony and Raphael were ready, they took off to find Blizzard.

"I hope we find him soon," Harmony called over her shoulder to her brother.

"We will find him," Raphael called back.

The two of them had been searching for about an hour when Harmony spotted something in the bushes. She dismounted from Tyson and walked over to the bushes. Harmony fell to her knees crying when she realised it was a collapsed Blizzard she had spotted. She called Raphael over to where Blizzard was lying. "You will have to get Father to bring the horsebox. There is no way we are walking him home like this," Harmony cried.

Raphael turned Spring and set off at a gallop. The whole way home he was trying to go as fast as he could. When he got back to the stable-yard everyone was still stood next to the horsebox.

"Where is Harmony?" Maurice asked.

"She is still with Blizzard," Raphael said, who was still trying to get his breath back after racing home.

"Well, what is the problem?" Maurice asked impatiently.

Raphael looked at his father. "We need the horsebox. Blizzard is in such a bad way that we cannot walk him home. We all need to go so that we can move him."

Maurice walked past everyone heading for the tack room.

"Father, where are you going?" Raphael asked.

"I am going to get my gun from the office. If Blizzard is as bad as you make it sound, it may be kinder to shoot him." Maurice then made his way into the office to fetch his gun.

While everyone got in the horsebox, Raphael put Spring in his stable. At that moment he could imagine his sister's reaction to their father trying to shoot Blizzard even though it could be the only option. As soon as he joined everyone in the horsebox they all set off to pick up Blizzard.

Meanwhile out in the woods, Harmony was sat next to Blizzard cuddling his neck and sobbing uncontrollably. "Please hold on, Blizzard. We will get you home soon," she whispered. She kept listening out for the horsebox hoping that it would arrive soon.

In the horsebox, Raphael was directing his father to where Blizzard was lying, hoping the horsebox was not too big to reach him. As they made their way through the lanes there were a few tight spots where everyone had to guide Maurice through the obstacles.

Harmony felt like she had been sat for hours waiting for help to arrive, when suddenly she heard the horsebox in the distance. Harmony got up from the ground, relieved that help had finally arrived. "They are here, Blizzard. We will have you in your stable in no time." She moved to stand in a place where the boys would see her.

When Maurice stopped the horsebox everyone jumped out, and Harmony led them straight to where Blizzard had collapsed. As they approached, Blizzard lifted his head slightly off the ground.

Maurice looked down at Blizzard, assessing the horse. After looking at him he made his decision. He walked back to the horsebox to retrieve his gun. As he started to walk back to the horse, Harmony spotted the gun. "Father, why do you have your gun?"

"The kindest thing we can do for him is to end it now," Maurice replied.

"We need to get him home. I do not want to lose him," Harmony told them.

"I am sorry, Harmony, but I have to do this," he told her.

"Please let me try to help him. If he gets worse in the night, then you can end it, but please let me try," Harmony begged.

"It will be over quickly for him. He will not know anything about it," Maurice informed her.

"Ask yourself, what would Mother do?" Harmony asked.

Maurice stood thinking for a moment as he knew exactly what his wife would have done. "Okay. You can try to help him through the night, but if he is still like this in the morning, I will end it."

Amos followed Pixel to the back of the horsebox. They gently lowered the ramp before heading back to the group to decide a plan of action.

"To do this we are going to have to think carefully about where we put people. I think we should have Harmony at his head to keep him calm. If we have Raphael helping Pixel to support his hind legs that will then leave me with Amos to support his front legs," Maurice instructed.

Harmony went to the horsebox to grab a head collar before running back to the boys, not wanting to waist any more time.

"I will try to pull him up so you guys can support him, but please be careful of his bad leg," Harmony ordered. She put the head collar on Blizzard before slowly pulling him up.

As soon as Blizzard started to get up, everyone moved into position ready to support him. They all started walking Blizzard slowly towards the horsebox. Harmony was more nervous than she had ever been. Even more nervous than when she was at patrol rider try-outs. Blizzard walked gingerly forwards finding it quite difficult to move.

"We will be in the horsebox soon, boy," Harmony reassured him.

The boys helped the horse up the ramp and into the horsebox. As soon as he was in, Blizzard collapsed again. Harmony gasped in fright. The boys walked down the ramp to where she was standing.

"What are we going to do with Tyson?" Harmony asked.

"I will ride him back," Raphael answered.

Now that her own horse had a way of getting back home, Harmony walked up the ramp to sit with Blizzard without discussing it with anyone. Maurice and Amos closed the ramp of the horsebox before climbing in the front with Pixel. To make the journey less bumpy for Blizzard, they took a slow steady drive home.

Maurice parked the horsebox as close to the stables as possible. He helped Amos lower the ramp of the horsebox then waited for Harmony to come out. When she never moved he walked up the ramp to her. Maurice knelt down next to his daughter before putting a sympathetic hand on her shoulder. "Look, Harmony, do not be surprised if he does not make it through the night. He is an old horse, and as a result, this is putting a lot of strain on his body," Maurice told her.

When Raphael finally got back, he put Tyson in a stable before helping the others move Blizzard to a stable. Once he was in the stable Harmony put a couple of rugs over him. After the big move, Blizzard's legs once again gave out.

Maurice stood watching as his daughter sat down next to his wife's horse.

"Father, I am going to stay with him tonight. I do not want him to be on his own if he dies," Harmony explained.

Maurice leaned on the stable door. "You should be the one getting some sleep. You have got your duty as head patrol rider tomorrow," he reminded her.

"I know, but right now the most important thing is Blizzard. Mother was on her own when she died. I do not want him to be on his own too," Harmony explained.

Maurice smiled. "You sound just like your mother."

All the boys except for Raphael went back to the cottage to get warm and have something to eat as they were now starving.

Raphael untacked Tyson before leaving him in the stable for the night. While he was sorting out Tyson, his sister was starting to settle down for the night. She quietly lay down next to Blizzard. "It's okay, boy, you are going to be fine. You just need to get some rest," she reassured him, even though it seemed like she was trying to reassure herself. She fell asleep with her head on the horse's neck.

Raphael checked on his sister before going to the cottage. He walked in the backdoor to find everyone sat at the kitchen table eating bread and cheese. He joined them at the table picking up his own piece of bread along with a chunk of cheese.

"How is she?" Amos asked.

"She is asleep with her head on Blizzard's neck," Raphael said.

"I hope Blizzard pulls through. Harmony will be devastated if he does not," Amos told them thoughtfully.

Maurice got up from the table. "Well you three, it is time we got to bed," he informed them.

"There is nothing more we can do except wait and hope for good news in the morning," Amos added.

As everyone left the kitchen Pixel had a thought. "Where am I going to sleep tonight?"

"You may sleep in Harmony's room for tonight," Maurice replied.

With the sleeping arrangements sorted they all went upstairs to bed. Although they all fell asleep quickly, Raphael and Pixel kept waking up thinking about Harmony out in the stable with Blizzard.

The next morning the boys were up early to help Harmony prepare for her first duty as head patrol rider.

At the stable-yard Harmony also woke up early, eager to see how Blizzard was doing. She sat up and then turned to face him. "Good morning, Blizzard. How are you feeling this morning?"

The first thing she noticed was that he did not appear to be moving. "Blizzard?" Harmony called quietly hoping he was just sleeping.

When he failed to move, she called his name a bit louder, but with no response from the horse it was clear that he had died during the night. Harmony quickly ran to the bottom of the garden. "RAPHAEL!" she shouted out.

When she could not see him coming she called his name again. She then spotted her brother running out of the cottage.

"What is the matter?" Raphael asked.

"It is Blizzard," she said as she turned to run back to his stable.

Raphael decided to run after her, sensing that something was wrong. When he got to the stable his sister was knelt beside Blizzard stroking his neck. Harmony looked up at her brother with tears rolling down her cheeks. "He has gone," she told him.

"Oh, Harmony, I am so sorry," Raphael said sympathetically and then knelt down beside his sister and hugged her. "You had better say your last goodbyes as we need to get you back to the cottage to get ready."

"Okay, can you give me a moment alone with him?" she asked.

"Sure," Raphael replied. He gave his sister one last hug before getting up and leaving the stable.

"Goodbye, Blizzard. I am going to miss you so much," Harmony told him and then started to cry again. She stroked him one last time before getting up. She walked over to the stable door then looked at the horse one more time before leaving. Once she was out of the stable Harmony looked up at her brother. "Could you grab my stuff from the cottage while I get Spring ready?" she asked.

"Okay. We do not have long though, as we need to leave to get you there on time," Raphael said.

Harmony walked off to get Spring ready, so Raphael made his way back to the cottage. When he walked into the kitchen he leaned up against the worktop thinking about how upset his sister was about losing Blizzard. Raphael was stood thinking when the others came down. The three of them sat at the table.

"How is Blizzard this morning?" Maurice asked.

Raphael looked down at the worktop before turning around to answer him. "He died during the night."

Amos and Pixel were shocked by the news.

"Is Harmony alright?" Amos asked.

Raphael turned his back to them, remembering his sister's reaction. "No. She is very upset. She has lost her last connection to our mother."

"Is Harmony nearly ready to go?" Maurice asked.

"Yes. She had started getting Spring ready when I left. I just need to grab her stuff from her room and then we can go to the stable-yard," Raphael said.

After he left, everyone got up from the table and went to the boot room to put their cloaks and boots on. Raphael had not been gone long when he came back down with some spare clothes for Harmony. Once they were wrapped up, they all went to the stable-yard.

At the stables Harmony was putting the finishing touches to Spring when the boys arrived.

"Good morning," Harmony greeted the boys.

"Good morning," everyone replied.

"We are ready to go when you are," Pixel told her.

Before she walked Spring over to the horsebox she took one last look at Blizzard. "Goodbye, Blizzard. I will really miss you," she said softly, trying not to cry.

Harmony untied Spring and slowly walked him over to the horsebox. Raphael helped Amos lower the ramp allowing Harmony to load him into it. After everyone had secured themselves in the horsebox, they started the journey to Elveshire Castle.

"Are you okay, Harmony? It must have been horrible waking up to discover that Blizzard had died in the night," Amos said.

"I do not want to talk about it."

"I just wanted to know if you were alright after finding Blizzard," Amos whispered.

"She just told you that she would rather not talk about it," Pixel shouted.

Amos turned to Pixel. "I was just asking her a question," Amos shouted back.

Pixel turned to Amos. "You know she gets upset when you talk about him, yet you just carry on," Pixel shouted.

"Will you two stop it?" Harmony shouted.

"Sorry," Amos apologised.

"Sorry," Pixel apologised as well.

For the rest of the journey Maurice and Raphael were discussing where to bury Blizzard.

"We don't have much further to go," Maurice announced.

Harmony was glad as she was not sure how much more of the discussion about Blizzard she could handle.

CHAPTER TWENTY-TWO

When they arrived at the castle the other patrol riders had only just arrived. Maurice parked the lorry then they all got out.

"Where are you going, Pixel? You should not be sneaking around," Harmony said.

"I have got to get to work," Pixel replied.

Harmony turned to Pixel. "You work in the castle?" she asked surprised.

"Not exactly," Pixel said, and then ran off into the castle leaving Harmony confused.

Harmony turned her attention back to her family. "Let us get Spring ready and then I will put my uniform on."

Raphael unloaded Spring and tied him to the horsebox. Harmony got Spring ready while the boys stood watching her. When Spring was ready, Harmony went into the horsebox to change into her uniform. While she was getting changed the boys put away the equipment that was no longer needed.

Harmony came out of the horsebox in a pair of black jodhpurs, long black riding boots, an ivory shirt covered by a burgundy tail jacket, with gold buttons and a black velvet riding hat. She stood on the steps showing them her uniform before making her way over to her family. "Well, Father, I guess I will see you in a week." Harmony walked over and gave him a quick hug. She then gave the other two longer hugs. As she untied Spring, Harmony thought of something. "I've just had a thought. Could you say goodbye to Blizzard for me and tell him how much I love him?" she asked.

"I will," Raphael replied.

Harmony mounted on to Spring. "Okay, patrol riders, mount up. I need you to line up next to each other as the royal family will be out soon," Harmony instructed.

The patrol riders mounted up and then lined up next to each other with Harmony in the middle. They had just finished getting ready as the king and queen's carriage pulled into the driveway.

In front of the carriage was a row of five young men. One of the young men was Pixel. Harmony looked to see if anyone else looked familiar. After she looked along the row once she noticed Goliath. She then noticed the three young men from town. They were on horseback in a uniform.

Harmony turned to the patrol riders. "We are to slot in between the princes and the carriage," she informed them.

They slotted into the gap behind the young men in front of the carriage. After everyone had got in position, they walked forwards towards the gates. Once they were through the gates they started trotting along the road.

Maurice, Amos and Raphael were stood next to the horsebox talking about Harmony.

"Father, I do not think she is ready for this. When she asked us to say goodbye to Blizzard for her she had tears in her eyes."

Maurice looked at the two boys. "Did either of you know Pixel was a prince?" he asked.

"No," the boys answered.

Back on the ride, Pixel turned in the saddle to see if Harmony felt okay. He could tell straight away that she still felt unhappy. Pixel asked Marko to switch places with Harmony so that she would be next to him. Marko happily switched places allowing Harmony to ride alongside Pixel.

"Are you alright?" he asked.

Harmony started crying. "I cannot stop thinking about Blizzard."

Goliath looked at Harmony. "Why? What happened to Blizzard?"

Harmony started crying even more, so Pixel answered his brother's question. "He died last night."

Suddenly realising something, Harmony pointed from Pixel to Goliath. "How do you two know each other?" she asked.

"Goliath is my older brother," Pixel answered.

Harmony sat trying to piece the puzzle together. "If Goliath is your older brother, then that would make you... Prince Pixel," she stated surprised.

"You are right although I—" Pixel started to say before being interrupted.

"How could you keep it from me?" Harmony asked quietly yet sounding angry. She had interrupted Pixel before he had finished explaining why he had not told her about being a prince. All Harmony wanted to do now was get away from Pixel. She kicked Spring into a fast trot until she found softer ground and then she galloped out of sight.

"What is going on with her?" Goliath asked as they watched Harmony disappear.

"I do not know but I need to find out," Pixel said.

It did not take Goliath long to realise what his brother was planning to do. "You cannot just ride off... Mother will go mad," he warned Pixel.

"I know. I just hope Harmony does not get hurt," Pixel explained.

Gilderoy looked at his two older brothers. "I will go and find her. Mother is always mad at me anyway so at least this time it will be for a good reason," he told them, and before his brothers could say anything, he took off.

They had been riding for so long it was starting to get dark. As it was darker in the woods Harmony struggled to see her surroundings. She had now put her trust entirely in Spring. Harmony was riding along when suddenly a tree branch hit her on her head. As she fell unconscious she slid off Spring's back. Spring stopped after she had fallen to the ground then stood by her side waiting for someone to find them.

When Gilderoy reached the place Harmony had vanished from he slowed down then started calling her name. After calling her name a few times he heard a horse whinnying in the distance. To make sure he called Harmony's name again. This time when the horse whinnied Cobalt whinnied back.

Now Gilderoy knew where he needed to go, he headed into the woods. Just like Harmony he had to put his trust in his horse. To help him stay on the right track he kept calling Harmony's name to keep the other horse whinnying.

After ten minutes of searching they came across a horse that was lying down. Gilderoy dismounted from Cobalt to take a closer look. On the horse he discovered a saddle with two saddlebags attached. He opened them up to see what was inside.

In the second bag he found what he needed – a torch. He switched the torch on and in the light he could see it was Harmony's horse. Using the torchlight he looked for any sign of injury on the horse. As he walked around Spring he found Harmony unconscious next to him. Knowing he needed to get back to his family he was sure of one thing, it was not going to be easy to do it alone.

First, he had to get Spring to stand up so he could lift Harmony on to his back. After putting Harmony in place he mounted on to Cobalt. He held Spring's reins then made his way back through the woods aided by the torchlight. As he neared the road he could hear hooves approaching. He came out of the trees to see his brothers heading towards him.

When Goliath got to his brother he stopped. As it was dark they could not see Harmony on Spring's back. It was not until Spring turned sideways they saw her in the torchlight. When they saw Harmony was unconscious Pixel, Goliath and Trixie dismounted.

Goliath took hold of Spring's reins while Gilderoy dismounted from Cobalt. Trixie held the horses while the boys dealt with Harmony and Spring. Pixel and Goliath gently slid Harmony off his back and onto the ground. During the whole process Spring stood still to make it easier for them.

As the two brothers stepped away from Harmony, Spring pulled his reins out of Gilderoy's hand. While they decided what to do with her, Spring started acting differently. Pixel decided to lay his cloak over Harmony to keep her warm, there was just one problem. Spring did not want to let anyone near her.

Trixie tried first followed by Goliath, but neither of them could get past him. Pixel tried again but Spring started rearing at him. He kept stamping his hooves warning people to stay away. Spring then turned his back end towards Goliath before laying his ears flat against his head.

"You had better get out of the way, Goliath. It looks like he is going to buck," Pixel warned his brother.

While the horse was distracted by Goliath, Pixel grabbed his reins. He then led the horse over to Gilderoy. While Gilderoy had Spring distracted, Pixel managed to lay his cloak over Harmony to keep her warm.

"I think we should get some human help. She has been unconscious for a while now," Pixel told them, sounding worried.

As Spring could sense how worried Pixel felt he became very restless. He once again tried to break free from Gilderoy's grasp.

Without waiting for anyone else's opinion, Pixel took his phone out of his pocket. He dialled 999 and then waited for someone to answer.

"Hello what service do you require?" the operator asked.

"I require an ambulance please," Pixel said, trying to remain calm.

"What is your current location?" the operator asked.

"We have been riding along the road from Elveshire Castle. We have been going straight heading north," Pixel replied.

"Okay, an ambulance is on its way," the operator informed him.

Pixel looked at Trixie. "We need to get the horses out of here."

Goliath and Gilderoy got back on their horses while Pixel walked over to Gilderoy. "Thank you for finding her for me," Pixel said to him thankfully.

"No problem, just glad I could put my rule-breaking to good use," Gilderoy replied.

Pixel walked back over to Harmony. "We will see you at the holiday home," he told his brothers.

The rest of the royal family carried on to their holiday home accompanied by the patrol riders and protectors. After they had left, Trixie tried to move Cleopatra, Spring and Shadow out of the way ready for the ambulance. Pixel had informed the ambulance that Harmony was unconscious, making it a higher priority emergency.

As Pixel looked down at Harmony, he noticed blood on her side. He decided to take a closer look to see what was causing it. He lifted her top to have a look at her ribs and discovered that the blood was seeping from a large gash on her side.

"How could I let this happen?" Pixel shouted frustrated. He then began to cry. "I am so sorry, Harmony. I should have followed you as soon as you took off."

Trixie walked over to where Pixel had knelt beside Harmony. "How about you go and stand with the horses to calm down," she suggested.

"Okay," Pixel replied. He got up and as he turned round, Trixie handed him the horse's reins. He then walked a short distance down the road. Pixel had not been gone long when Trixie spotted the ambulance approaching. Luckily, the ambulance did not have its siren on, allowing Pixel to return with the horses.

When Spring saw the ambulance approaching he found the stress of the situation too much to handle. Having anticipated Spring's reaction, Pixel clipped a lead rope to his bridle. Spring tried everything to break free from Pixel's grip.

The ambulance stopped by Harmony and then two paramedics quickly got out. One of the paramedics went into the back of the ambulance to grab their bag, while the second paramedic made his way over to Harmony. "How long has she been unconscious?" he asked.

"We are not sure exactly. She has been out for at least half an hour," Pixel answered.

"Do you know what happened?" the paramedic asked.

"We did not see it happen but judging by the gash on her side I would say she had a run in with a couple of trees," Pixel answered. He was doing his best to ignore Spring who had become very restless.

While the paramedics were getting Harmony ready to load into the ambulance, Trixie walked over to Pixel. He looked up at her so that they could discuss who was doing what. "You go in the ambulance with her. I will go to her house to let her family know what has happened."

Trixie made her way towards the ambulance ready to travel with her friend. While she waited for the paramedics she watched as Pixel tried to walk away with the horses but Spring would not budge. Pixel pulled hard on the lead rope hoping the horse would walk forward. Instead of moving forward, Spring decided to lie down. Knowing he had no chance of getting to the castle, Pixel took his phone out of his pocket. He called one of the stable-hands at the castle.

"I need you to bring a horsebox to pick me up. If you drive along the route to the holiday home you will spot me stood with three horses," he explained. Pixel put his phone down just as the paramedics were getting ready to load Harmony into the back of the ambulance. As Pixel started walking towards the ambulance, Spring stood up.

"Which one of you is coming with her?" the paramedic asked.

"Trixie," Pixel answered.

Trixie looked at Pixel confused.

"You cannot handle Spring when he is like this," Pixel told her.

Trixie climbed into the ambulance while Pixel walked the horses away. He turned around to watch the ambulance drive out of sight. Spring started whinnying after Harmony as the ambulance disappeared out of sight.

"I know, I miss her too," Pixel told him comfortingly while stroking him.

Pixel started pacing, getting impatient for the horsebox to arrive.

CHAPTER TWENTY-THREE

It was completely dark when Pixel noticed two headlights heading towards him. The horsebox slowed as it approached. The stable-hand stopped the horsebox before climbing out. "Good evening, sir," the stable-hand greeted Pixel.

Pixel bowed his head in acknowledgement. He followed the stable-hand to the back of the horsebox. The two of them loaded the horses into the horsebox before beginning the journey to Harmony's cottage to tell her family of her accident.

On the journey back to the cottage Pixel was thinking, wondering how Harmony's father would react to her being in a human hospital after falling off Spring. When he arrived at the cottage he entered the kitchen, where he saw the boys sitting round the table.

Raphael looked up, surprised to see Pixel stood in the doorway. "What are you doing here?"

"I am afraid I have some bad news. Harmony is in a human hospital," he said nervously.

"Why is she in hospital?" Raphael asked.

"She has got a deep cut over her ribs. The paramedics think she might have cracked a rib. The last time I saw her she was also unconscious."

Maurice looked at Pixel. "Why did you take my daughter to humans?" he asked.

Luckily, Pixel had prepared himself for Maurice's reaction, which helped him stay calm. "It was her only chance to get help. If I had not, she could have died."

"Well from what my father said to her recently, he would be happy for her to be dead," Raphael said.

"What are you talking about?" Pixel asked confused.

"I will explain later. Right now, we need to be with Harmony," Raphael said.

They left the cottage to go to the hospital. The only person missing was Maurice. Raphael drove to the hospital as fast he could, wanting to get to his sister. On the journey he realised something. "Who travelled in the ambulance with her?" he asked.

"Trixie, Harmony's friend and fellow patrol rider," Pixel answered.

Raphael pulled into the hospital carpark looking for a space when he spotted one by the entrance of the hospital. He parked the horsebox then everyone climbed out wanting to see Harmony.

When they entered the hospital Pixel spotted Trixie sat in the waiting area. "Hello, Trixie. What is the latest information?" he asked.

Trixie looked nervously at the two boys with Pixel. "She woke up in the ambulance on the way here. Once they got her in the hospital they took her off for some tests, and that is all I know. They could not give me anymore information because I am not family."

Wanting to know more, Pixel led the way over to the reception desk. "Hello. We are here to see Harmony Redvers."

"Are you related to her?"

"I am her boyfriend. They are her brother and her cousin," Pixel said.

The receptionist looked at each of the boys. "I am afraid we are only letting one person in at a time to see her."

"Raphael, you go in with her; you are her brother," Pixel insisted.

The four of them looked back at the receptionist.

"Okay. She is in the third room off that corridor," she explained, pointing to a corridor on the right.

"Thank you," Raphael said thankfully. He walked along the corridor until he got to the room with Harmony in it. He nervously walked into the room then slowly sat in the chair next to Harmony's bed. "Hello, Harmony, it is me Raphael. Harmony, you need to wake up, we all need you, especially Spring. He has not been acting right since the accident. When you pull through this we will ride the horses on the beach. Please wake up."

At the sound of her brother's voice, Harmony opened her eyes. "Is that you, Raphael?"

"Of course it is. Pixel, Amos and Trixie are out in the waiting area."

Harmony turned her head to face away from her brother. "I did not mean to run away from them. It is just I was upset about Blizzard and then I found out that Pixel is actually a prince, and I was angry at him for that."

"Pixel is a prince?" Raphael asked bewildered.

Harmony turned her head to look at her brother. "Yes, he is. You mean he never told you?"

"No, he never told us, not even when he told us what had happened to you."

"You do not mind that he is related to Goliath?" Harmony asked.

"Come on, Harmony, you would never say those two are related. Pixel is nothing like Goliath. Pixel is kind, thoughtful and caring. He also loves you and cares about you more than anyone. He proved that today."

"I know, and I really love him too. It is just, is this the life I really want to live? I have always wanted to be with Damien. To live amongst humans the way my whole childhood had been." She then noticed her brother's expression. "I would stick to the elvish rules. I would just have fun with the humans at the same time."

Raphael could tell his sister was worried about his reaction to her plans. "I think it is great that you want to do something with your life. I always wish that I had done something with mine when I had the chance. Father needs more looking after than he is letting on. I do not think he will ever be the same again. Mother's death changed him a lot," Raphael told her.

After they had finished talking, the doctor entered the room and walked over to Harmony's bed. "How do you feel?" he asked.

Harmony looked up at him. "I feel fine apart from my ribs being a bit sore." She was beginning to wonder how many times the doctors and nurses could ask the same question.

"If you still feel fine in an hour, it will be okay for you to go home," the doctor explained.

"Is it okay if she goes for a walk?" Raphael asked.

"I would rather she didn't yet. We just want to make sure she gets through this hour without any problems."

"Can the others come and see me?" Harmony asked.

"I will send them in," the doctor said and then left the room.

Harmony looked at her brother when the doctor had left. "At least I do not have to stay in overnight," she said happily.

"When did you regain consciousness?" Raphael asked.

"I came around in the ambulance on the journey here."

The room was quiet when Amos, Trixie and Pixel entered.

"Hello," Harmony greeted them.

"How are you feeling?" Amos asked, walking over to the bed.

"I am feeling fine. It is just my ribs stopping me from running out of here."

Everyone chuckled and then Pixel walked over to the bed. Amos walked over to Trixie to give Pixel some room.

"When are they letting you out of here?" Pixel asked.

"The doctor told us that if she still feels okay in an hour it will be fine for her to go home," Raphael answered.

With everyone in the room the hour seemed to pass by quickly. As the doctor approached the room Trixie, Amos and Pixel left to wait for them in the waiting area. Not long after they left the doctor entered the room. "All your tests came back clear. You may feel sore due to cuts and bruises but you were lucky to avoid broken bones. So, do you feel okay?" the doctor asked.

"I certainly do," Harmony said.

The doctor looked at Raphael then back at Harmony. "Well I can't see any reason why you can't go home. Just take it easy this evening okay," he instructed, and then left the room.

"I will leave you to get dressed then," Raphael said.

"Okay, just wait outside the door for me," Harmony instructed.

While Raphael waited outside for his sister to get dressed, he thought about her relationship with Pixel. He had hoped she would find an elf she liked at the try-outs, yet he never imagined it would actually happen. It also made him happy that she had made a new friend in Trixie.

Harmony walked out of the room carrying her medication. The two of them walked side by side along the corridor to the waiting area. Raphael kept to his sister's pace as best as he could, even though it seemed slow to him he never complained.

When the others spotted them coming along the corridor they got up from their seats. Together they walked over to Harmony and Raphael to find out what was happening.

"Is that it?" Pixel asked.

"Yes it is. We can now head home," Raphael answered.

All five of them walked out of the hospital glad to be heading home, no one seemed happier than Harmony to be leaving. Everyone climbed into the horsebox with Raphael driving. Harmony told her brother to drive carefully as her ribs were still tender.

"While we are on the subject, I think when we get home after dropping Trixie off you three should get out before I drive down the bumpy track," Raphael suggested.

They dropped Trixie off at her house. Before she went indoors they each wished her a merry Christmas. She wished them a merry Christmas back before closing the door of the horsebox. Raphael pulled away from the cottage heading home.

CHAPTER TWENTY-FOUR

When the horsebox arrived outside the cottage, Amos, Pixel and Harmony got out. The three of them watched as Raphael drove down the track into the darkness. As they turned to face the cottage ready to enter, Harmony noticed something missing. "Where are my pretty icicle lights that get put up every year?" she asked.

"Still in a box in the cupboard I think," Amos said, knowing that Raphael would be in trouble when he returned.

Harmony opened the front door, which did not have its wreath hanging on it, before entering the warmth of the cottage followed by Pixel and Amos. At this point Harmony gave up hope that the decorations would have been put up inside. As they walked in to the cottage Maurice was sat in his favourite wingback chair.

"Look, Maurice. Harmony is home," Amos said cheerfully.

Maurice said nothing. He would not even look at his daughter.

Harmony walked over to the sideboard beside her. She opened the top drawer and pulled out a folder filled with papers. As Harmony walked back to where she had been standing Maurice stood up and looked at her. "I want you to move out as soon as possible," he told her.

"Fine, give me a week and I will leave after Christmas," Harmony said.

Pixel gave Harmony a gentle hug. "I had better get back to my family," he informed her.

"You do not have to leave, Pixel. You are more than welcome to stay here," Maurice told him.

Pixel looked at Maurice. "I had better spend Christmas with my family. I will then go with Harmony because I am going to stick by her no matter what," he pointed out. Pixel gave Harmony one last cuddle before leaving the cottage.

When Raphael entered the living room he could see his sister was not happy.

"Why are my Christmas decorations not up?" Harmony asked.

"I will start on them now," Raphael replied. He knew it was the only way he could make up for not having them up already.

"I would like the blue and white icicle lights up outside. The tree can be placed in the corner by the window. Each of the windows needs a candle arch placed in it. One garland around the front door with the other going around the mantelpiece. Wreath on the door, stockings hung on the fireplace, Christmas cards up, then I think we will be done," Harmony instructed.

Raphael could not believe how much his sister wanted him to do. He looked at Amos hoping he had no plans to head home anytime soon.

"I will decorate the tree," Harmony told him when she saw her brother's expression.

Raphael walked up the stairs with Amos to get the decorations from the spare bedroom. Harmony followed them to put the folder of papers in her bedroom, she then made her way to the spare bedroom.

Before Harmony reached the spare room, Raphael made sure there was nothing for her to carry. Not that there were that many decorations anyway. Harmony followed the boys down the stairs carrying a bag containing some of the tree decorations. Raphael put the tree up in the corner first so Harmony could start decorating it.

The colour scheme throughout the decorations were the traditional red, gold and green, the only exception being the blue and white icicle lights outside.

Amos helped Raphael with the outside lights while Harmony tackled most of the decorations indoors. Maurice sat watching his family get into the Christmas spirit, not wanting anything to do with Christmas.

"Father, are you coming with us to the church carol service this year?" Harmony asked.

"Absolutely not," Maurice answered sternly.

"When is it?" Amos asked. He had come in to get the wreath for the front door.

"It is in the evening on Christmas Eve," Harmony replied.

"Rhoda and I will go. There is nothing better than singing traditional carols on Christmas Eve," Amos told her lovingly.

Harmony handed Amos the wreath then he left the cottage to hang it on the front door. Harmony hung the stockings above the fireplace before stepping back to admire her work. The cottage had almost been completely decorated and only a few decorations remained but Harmony knew Raphael would get angry if she tried to put them up herself.

When Amos and Raphael entered the cottage she got them to put up the decorations she could not.

Maurice got up from his chair, then Harmony looked at the clock to discover it was time for her father to put the horses in their stables. She then stood back to admire the festive looking room.

When the boys came down they complemented Harmony on her work. Harmony then remembered one thing she had not been able to do. She handed the star to her brother. He reached up placing the star on top of the Christmas tree. The three of them looked at each other and smiled.

"I had better get home," Amos told them.

"Will we see you tomorrow?" Harmony asked.

Amos gave her a hug. "Probably, now I want you to take it easy." He then turned to Raphael. "See you tomorrow," he said and then left the cottage.

"Well I had better go and start packing," Harmony said with a sigh.

"Why do you need to pack?" Raphael asked.

"Father told me that I have to move out."

Knowing the news would make her brother angry, Harmony decided to go and start packing. After she had left the living room, Raphael went out to the kitchen to wait for his father.

Harmony walked into her bedroom to start packing. She pulled her case out of her wardrobe and placed it on her bed before returning to her wardrobe. Before grabbing a load of clothes to put in her suitcase, Harmony considered what she would be wearing for the rest of that week. She looked at her clothes carefully choosing her outfits.

The outfits she chose to wear for the week were put to one side, allowing her to pick up lots of clothes at a time. Even though it made her side sore, Harmony did not care. She was actually pleased to be leaving. Once her suitcase had been filled with as many clothes as it could carry, she grabbed a couple of holdalls from under her bed. She knew she would not be able to take everything at once, but she wanted to take as much as she could.

Harmony then realised that she could not leave Tyson behind, therefore she grabbed the folder off her bed. She searched through it until she found her horse's papers and then placed the papers on top of the clothes in her suitcase.

Time had passed quicker than Harmony had realised, for that reason she decided to leave the rest of the packing until the next spare moment she had. She changed into her nightwear ready to get into bed. After getting changed, it occurred to her there was a suitcase on her bed. She quietly slid the suitcase off, allowing her to get into bed. She climbed in then turned to face the wall.

Harmony had not been in bed long when Raphael came up to turn in for the night. On his way past he looked in his sister's room to find her tucked up in bed. Before he left the room he blew out the candle on her bedside table.

The next morning Harmony awoke to find it had turned out to be a cold crisp winter's morning. During the night there had been a dusting of snow which covered everything in a thin white blanket.

She stayed in bed, not wanting to leave her nice warm duvet. She was just lying there contemplating not getting out of bed for the entire day when there was a knock on her door. She ignored whoever it was, hoping they would leave her in peace.

"Come on, Harmony, you have to go Christmas shopping with Rhoda," Raphael reminded her.

"Why do you not do your own Christmas shopping?" Harmony asked.

"I have got to work with father; it is his busiest time of year."

"Fine, I am getting up," Harmony told him sounding unhappy at the prospect of leaving the warm duvet for the icy air outside. She heard her brother walk away so she got out of bed.

Harmony walked over to her wardrobe and picked out a dress to wear that her cousin Rhoda would approve of. As it felt cold she picked out a cloak too. Harmony put the clothes on the bed before walking over to her chest of drawers. From inside the drawers she grabbed a chemise to put under her dress.

After Harmony had put her dress on she made her way to the bathroom to have a wash. Once she felt awake and refreshed Harmony walked back to her bedroom to run a brush through her hair. As it was cold she decided to leave her hair down to keep her ears warm.

When she had checked her outfit would be acceptable for her cousin she went downstairs to grab some breakfast. She got herself a bowl of cereal before making her way over to the table. While Harmony sat eating her breakfast her thoughts drifted to everything she had to do before Christmas. Not only did she need to go to town with Rhoda, she also had many chores around the cottage that needed tackling as well as the stable-yard.

CHAPTER TWENTY-FIVE

Harmony had just finished clearing away all the breakfast things when Rhoda arrived. When Rhoda entered the room Harmony could tell her cousin was scrutinising her outfit.

"Are you ready to go?" Rhoda asked. She started walking through the cottage with Harmony following.

"I am ready to go," Harmony replied as she climbed in to the cart.

Rhoda set off, heading for Elvesbridge. "Have you got much to do this week?" she asked.

"I have got lots to do. Raphael and father are working really hard selling horses and getting the business stables up together leaving me everything that needs doing at home."

"What have you got to do?" Rhoda asked.

"Thoroughly clean the entire stable-yard. The worst job is having to take all the bedding out of the stables and starting again with fresh bedding. Clean the cottage from top to bottom, finish packing, do the baking and the food shopping." Harmony started to think that it would be way too much for one person to do in a week.

"Why do you not ask Pixel to help you?" Rhoda asked.

Harmony looked at her, surprised by her suggestion. "He probably has enough to do without me asking for help."

"I am sure he would do it for you."

"Amos told you about me kissing Pixel didn't he?" Harmony asked.

"Of course he did."

Harmony sat thinking about the moment she upset Damien by kissing Pixel. Rhoda looked at Harmony and she could tell something was on her mind. "What are you thinking about?" she asked.

"Just something that happened at patrol rider try-outs," Harmony replied.

"Do you want to talk about it?"

"I cannot."

"I will not tell anyone," Rhoda said.

Harmony thought about telling her, wondering if maybe she could give her some advice.

"What happened?" Rhoda asked.

"Damien came there."

Rhoda stopped the horse. "What?" she said sounding alarmed as she turned to look at Harmony.

"I was getting Spring ready when Damien appeared. He told me he had followed me. The two of us were stood talking when Pixel walked over to us. I told him Damien was my cousin. While Pixel and I were talking, Damien went in the horsebox to get Spring's tack. The next thing I know Pixel and I were kissing. I did not know that Damien had been watching. When Pixel and I broke apart, Damien practically threw Spring's tack at me and then ran off."

Rhoda got the horse moving before sitting in silence. Harmony became worried about what her cousin was thinking. Rhoda looked at Harmony. "Okay Harmony. I am going to be honest with you," she said.

"What about?" Harmony asked.

"You need to make a decision."

"What decision?"

Rhoda sighed. She could see why Maurice got frustrated with his daughter sometimes. "On Christmas Day you have got to leave home. You need to decide whether you are going to go back to the humans and try to make things right with Damien. Your other option is to stay in Elveshire with your birth family."

Finally, the two of them arrived in town, which pleased Harmony as she was not sure she could take anymore words of wisdom from her cousin. They took the horse to the town stables and then walked back to the shops to begin the shopping.

Harmony wanted to get the shopping done as quickly as possible as she wanted to get home and work on some more of her list. Harmony looked at Rhoda. "Have you got much to do this week?" she asked.

"Amos is taking care of the stables, so mother and I just have to clean the cottage and do the baking," Rhoda said.

Harmony liked the sound of a family working together but she knew there was no way her family would do the same.

The two of them walked into different shops gradually crossing things off their lists. After a while they split up to buy their presents for each other. Once all the shopping had been done they walked back to the town stables to get the horse and cart.

On their way they spotted Pixel with a couple of his brothers. Pixel waved so Harmony waved back. The two girls carried on walking except Harmony was now smiling. Rhoda watched as her cousin seemed to be thinking about something. "What are you thinking about?" she asked.

"I am making my decision on where I am going to live after Christmas Day."

At the stables the girls put their bags in the cart while the stable boy fetched their horse. After the horse had been hitched up to the cart, the girls climbed aboard to begin the journey home. Rhoda waited until they were out of town before she started speaking to Harmony. "Do you like Pixel?" she asked.

"He seems a nice enough young man," Harmony said.

"Do you like him enough to stay?" Rhoda asked.

"It would not matter if I did; he is a prince and I work for his family."

"Does that mean you have chosen the humans?"

"I do not know. I am still thinking about it," Harmony replied.

"Well, can I just say that if you went back to the humans, Amos and I would definitely miss you. I also know your brother would miss you too," Rhoda said.

Harmony did not say anything as she wanted to make her own decision in her own time. The only trouble was, time was running out.

After the conversation, the rest of the journey was silent. Harmony decided to use the rest of the time planning for the week ahead. She thought it would be a good idea to make a timetable for each day.

When they arrived at Harmony's cottage Harmony got down from the cart and grabbed her shopping from the back. She said goodbye to Rhoda and then watched as she drove away out of sight.

CHAPTER TWENTY-SIX

Harmony let herself in the front door before taking the shopping straight up to her bedroom in case anyone came home early. Before going back downstairs she grabbed a pen and a couple of pieces of paper. She walked down into the hall where she swapped her shoes for a pair of comfy slippers before going to the kitchen.

As the aga kept the kitchen nice and warm, she sat at the kitchen table ready to write a list of what needed to be done. At the top of the page she wrote 'jobs to do'. She then began listing each of the jobs down the page. Finish packing, clean the cottage, clean the stable-yard, wrap presents, do the food shopping and do the baking.

It was now lunchtime so Harmony made herself a sandwich before sitting back at the table. She looked at her list, thinking about what to do that afternoon. It then occurred to her to use the afternoon to do the smaller jobs.

Harmony cleared away her plate before going upstairs to change into her riding clothes. Even though she had other jobs to do she could not forget about the horses. She made her way to the stable-yard to muck out the stables. Before she went to the stables she stopped and looked at the horses in the field.

It was the first time she had seen all the horses together in the field since the loss of Blizzard. As she watched all the horses, tears began to fill her eyes remembering him. While she was stood at the gate someone walked over and joined her.

"Hello, Trixie," Harmony greeted her.

"Hello," Trixie said.

Harmony started walking away from the gate.

"Where are you going?" Trixie asked.

"I have got to muck out the stables before I can put that lot to bed."

"Would you like some help?"

"That would be nice," Harmony replied.

They walked to the yard together in silence. When they got to the stables the two girls got to work. They started by sorting out the hay nets and water buckets. While they were filling up the water buckets Trixie noticed her friend's mind seemed to be focused on something else.

"Are you okay?" Trixie asked.

"Yeah, fine," Harmony replied.

Trixie knew her friend would tell her what was on her mind when she was ready. Trixie started mucking out Pandora's stable so Harmony started mucking out Tyson's stable. The girls were working in silence. The next time they spoke to each other they were in the hay barn filling up hay nets.

"What were you thinking about earlier?" Trixie asked.

"Just thinking about something Rhoda said to me coming back from town. I guess she is right."

"What did she say?" Trixie asked.

"My father has asked me to move out at Christmas, therefore she told me now would be a good time to decide whether I want to go back to the humans or stay with the elves."

The two girls started carrying the filled hay nets back to the stables.

"Have you decided what you are going to do?" Trixie asked.

"There was once a time when the decision would have been easy, now I am not so sure," Harmony replied as she hung up the hay nets Trixie had filled. It had now started to get dark even though it was not that late.

"I had better be getting home," Trixie informed her.

"Thank you for helping me out this afternoon," Harmony said.

"No problem. I will see you at church on Christmas Eve," Trixie said.

"Okay, see you on Christmas Eve."

Trixie left so Harmony went to the tack room to get the horses' head collars. She got the horses in two at a time to get the job done faster. Once all the horses had been put in their stables she returned to the cottage.

Harmony walked in the back door to find Raphael sat at the table eating his tea.

"I put your tea in the oven to keep warm," Raphael informed her.

"Where is Father?" Harmony asked.

"He is in the living room wondering why you did not get more jobs done today."

Harmony looked towards the living room, annoyed that her father was being so hard on her. "What is his problem?" she asked.

"I am going to warn you now that he will probably try his hardest to make you as miserable as possible until you leave," Raphael said.

Harmony got her tea out of the oven before joining her brother at the table. "I just wanted this Christmas to be perfect. I wanted everyone to be happy and having fun," she told him.

"It would be nice but we both know that is not going to happen." Raphael got up from the table carrying his plate and cup over to the sink.

As he placed it on the side, Harmony noticed a big pile of washing-up in the sink. "Let me guess, I am on washing-up duty?" she asked.

"I am afraid so," Raphael replied. He left the kitchen leaving Harmony to eat her tea alone. After she had finished, she slowly got up to begin the mountain of washing-up.

By now she started to feel exhausted. Not knowing how much longer she could stay awake, Harmony cleaned the kitchen as quickly as possible. She closed the last cupboard pleased that the kitchen was clean and tidy.

Knowing she could not sit and relax in the living room there was only one place she wanted to go, to bed. Not wanting to say goodnight to her father, Harmony headed straight for the stairs.

When she reached the landing she looked over at her brother's bedroom to find the door shut. Harmony did not want to disturb him, so she made her way to her own bedroom.

As she looked across at her bedside table the candle had already been lit so it was not dark in the room. Harmony walked over to her window to look at the view, but it was too dark to see anything, so she shut the curtains.

After changing in to her more comfortable nightgown, Harmony snuggled under her duvet trying to get warm, while listening to the sounds around her. The day had been exhausting which helped Harmony drift off into a deep sleep.

CHAPTER TWENTY-SEVEN

For the rest of the week Harmony was kept busy with all the Christmas preparations. Raphael helped out when he could, however, Maurice seemed to make sure that his son did not have much spare time.

With three days until Christmas, Harmony was starting to fall behind so Rhoda went to the cottage to help with the cleaning and the baking. Even though Harmony enjoyed the help she knew her father would not be happy as he tried to keep her own brother from helping out.

The next day after seeing to the horses, Harmony decided to concentrate on getting the baking done. In the afternoon she needed to go into the village to get as much food as she could for the Christmas dinner.

That evening Maurice entered the kitchen followed by Raphael. "Where is our tea?" he demanded.

"I am just getting it out of the oven now," Harmony said. She walked over to the oven and took out a cottage pie. She carried it to the table before placing it in the middle. She then returned to the cooker for the vegetables. The last two things to be placed on the table were the bread and gravy.

"I hope you have been keeping up with your chores," Maurice told her.

"Of course, tomorrow I am spending some time in the village to get some of the food I could not get today," Harmony informed him.

The three of them sat at the table then began eating their tea. Raphael was glad they were eating in silence as there was so much tension in the air that he felt it would not take much for his sister and father to start arguing.

Once they had finished tea, Maurice left the table to go into the living room. Harmony and Raphael got up from the table knowing their father's mood would not change until Harmony left the cottage on Christmas day.

As it was Raphael's turn to put the horses in their stables he walked into the boot room leaving Harmony to wash up and dry up again. Luckily when she cooked, Harmony washed up as she went along not leaving much to do after they had eaten.

While she was stood at the sink washing up, Harmony started thinking about her decision. Right now, she felt like there was nothing for her with the elves. Yes, she had friends and family but she hardly ever got to spend time with them for fun. Her own father did not want her there, so she was finding it hard to think of a reason to stay with the elves when a better life was back with the humans.

Harmony was just finishing off in the kitchen when Raphael returned from the stables. When his sister did not notice him come in, he knew her mind was on something else. He closed the boot room door before walking over to her. "Are you okay?" Raphael asked.

"I am fine."

"What were you thinking about?"

"I was thinking about whether I am going to stay with the elves or go back to the humans when I leave on Christmas Day," she said.

"Why would you even consider going back to the humans?" Raphael asked.

"I miss it. The life I had there was so different to the life I have here. I loved being able to go out and have fun with my friends. I miss all the time the family spent together, and there did not have to be a reason for it."

"You have family and friends here," Raphael told her.

"It is not the same. The last two times I have seen Trixie was one was in the hospital and the second time she helped me muck out the stables. I would not call Freedom a friend, not after the way she treated me in our kitchen. Goliath, I never know where I stand with him. The other princes I like even though I don't know them that well."

"What about the rest of us?" Raphael asked.

"I think you know the answer to that," Harmony said.

"What are you going to do now?" he asked.

"I am going to go to bed. I think I might read my book for a little while, but I want an early night as tomorrow is Christmas Eve and I get the feeling it is going to be a busy day." As she left the kitchen she was glad she had spoken to her brother because she always found that it helped her with her thoughts.

CHAPTER TWENTY-EIGHT

The next morning seemed to start off quite peaceful and relaxed but Harmony knew that it would not stay that way. She looked out of her bedroom window to see her father and brother heading off to work.

Knowing there was a lot to get done, Harmony climbed out of bed. Not wanting to spend all day at the stables, Harmony decided to go into the village to pick up the food they would need for the next day as well as a few other bits for the cottage.

Harmony had put on one of her dresses so she put a cloak over the top before leaving the cottage to keep warm. The cloak shielded her from the brisk breeze as she walked along the snow-covered path to the stables.

As the journey would be into the village, Harmony decided to get Conker the cart horse in from the field. She was standing at the field gate hoping the horse would come to her if she called it. "Conker," she called out to the horse.

The horse carried on grazing, completely ignoring Harmony. Determined that her cloak and dress were not going to get dirty, Harmony called the horse's name again. "Conker," she called out again, hoping it would work this time.

The horse looked up, so Harmony called it over to her. "Come on, Conker."

Conker made her way over to the gate making it possible for Harmony to put her head collar on without getting dirty. She let the horse out of the field leading her to the stable-yard and then quickly brushed the horse over before putting her harness on.

After hitching the horse up to the cart Harmony started the journey to Willowsbury. During the quiet journey she thought about what she needed from the village, but her mind then began wandering to what she was going to do about leaving the next day.

The first thought that popped into her mind was that she wanted to go back to the humans, to her that was home. One problem with that idea was that she was sure by now Damien would have told everyone what she did to him, meaning there would be a high possibility that no one would want to talk to her.

When she started thinking about living with the elves it was a different problem. She had plenty of people talking to her, but she did not have anywhere to stay. Unlike with the humans she had not known the elves long enough for someone to offer her a place to stay.

Before Harmony had a chance to realise how long she had been travelling, she arrived in Willowsbury and was making her way to the village stables where Conker would be staying while Harmony did her shopping.

The first stop was the village shop where she could get all the ingredients she would need for the large amount of baking that needed to be done that afternoon. As Harmony went to leave the shop the shopkeeper wished her a merry Christmas.

"Merry Christmas," Harmony returned.

Next she decided to go to the greengrocer to get the vegetables for the Christmas dinner. While she was there she got some fresh fruit for the fruit bowl as well as some apples and carrots for the horses. As she left the greengrocers they wished her a merry Christmas so she wished them a merry Christmas in return.

Wanting to leave the butchers until last, because the meat would be the heaviest to carry, Harmony had to decide between the bakers or the florists. She was stood deciding which way to go when she spotted Pixel's brothers riding through the village.

When Gilderoy spotted Harmony stood in the street he rode over to her as he had not seen her since the accident in the woods. He looked down at her waiting for her to look up at him.

"Good morning, Harmony. How are you feeling?" he asked.

"Good morning, Gilderoy. I am still a bit bruised and sore but apart from that I am fine."

"I am glad to hear that and I am sure my brothers will be too."

"I have never had the chance before therefore I would like to say thank you for coming after me. I know it was wrong of me to run off in the first place, but thank you," Harmony said.

"No problem, I was just glad I had been able to find you." Gilderoy looked up to see his brothers were now stood with Goliath. "I had better go... still lots to do before tomorrow," he explained.

"Okay, goodbye, Gilderoy."

"Goodbye, Harmony." Gilderoy rode off to where the rest of the princes were standing.

As Harmony watched, she could see the other princes stood looking at her while they were talking. Starting to feel uncomfortable, she decided to go into the bakers to get a loaf of bread to go with the stew they were having for tea.

Harmony was glad she had almost completed her shopping. First, she visited the florist where she picked up a bunch of holly and a sprig of mistletoe, as well as a few bunches of flowers. Her final stop was the butchers where she picked up the turkey for the Christmas dinner along with some mini sausages wrapped in bacon. While she was there she also picked up the beef for the stew that night.

"Are you ready for tomorrow?" the butcher asked.

"Not yet, but hopefully everything will be done in time," Harmony replied.

The butcher handed her the meat wrapped in paper before she paid him. While the butcher sorted out the change, Harmony put the meat in her basket. The butcher handed Harmony her change before wishing her a merry Christmas.

"Merry Christmas," Harmony replied before leaving the butcher's shop.

When Harmony stepped out of the shop she looked to the end of the street to find the princes had gone. She was glad they were gone because she could get to the village stables without being stopped.

In the stables Conker had already been placed in her harness. While the horse was being taken care of, Harmony placed her shopping in the cart. Once Conker had been securely hitched up Harmony climbed aboard thanking the stable lad as she left, making her way home.

When she arrived at the stable-yard she stopped Conker and climbed down from the cart. She backed the horse up so the cart would be in the cart barn out of the weather. Harmony took Conker's harness off before putting her out in the field with the other horses.

CHAPTER TWENTY-NINE

Harmony grabbed the shopping from the cart before making her way back to the cottage. She placed the shopping basket on the table before unpacking the contents.

Not wanting to get her going-out dress dirty, Harmony changed into a dress that she wore for doing chores around the cottage. She also tied her hair up to keep it out of the way. She also hoped that by tying it up she would not need to wash it before the carol service.

With her work clothes on, Harmony made her way to the kitchen to make a start on the baking. She decided to start by making the mince pies. When they had been put in the oven she started on the cookies to hang on the Christmas tree as well as the gingerbread house. While she worked on the gingerbread she heard the boot room door open causing her to look up. She looked over to the door to see Gilderoy leaning his back up against the doorframe.

"What are you doing here?" Harmony asked.

"Pixel wanted to come himself but he had to help mother and father with arrangements for the ball," Gilderoy replied.

"Oh. Why was Pixel coming?"

"He wanted to tell you that if you wanted to, our parents have agreed that you can live at our castle. It will be in the servants' quarters but you will get to spend all day with the horses."

Harmony could not believe it. It was like it was a sign that she was meant to stay with the elves.

"Harmony, are you okay?" Gilderoy asked.

"I am now. I had started to think I would not have anywhere to go tomorrow."

"Is that a yes?"

"Yes. I would like to move in to the castle."

Gilderoy reached into his pocket before holding his hand out to Harmony with an envelope in it.

"What is this?" Harmony asked, taking the envelope from him.

"It is your invite to the ball tomorrow evening."

"Wait, what? I cannot go to a ball."

"Why can you not attend?" Gilderoy asked.

"I do not have a dress for starters, and I have no clue how to act around the royal family."

"The dress is taken care of and you get on fine with my brothers and I," Gilderoy said reassuringly.

"What do you mean 'the dress is taken care of'?" Harmony asked.

Gilderoy chuckled. "You will find out tomorrow."

Knowing she was not going to get the answer she was looking for, Harmony decided to tackle the other subject. "I know I get on well with you and your brothers, but it will be different around your parents and grandparents."

"We will help you." Gilderoy walked over to the boot room door. "I had better get back to the castle, as there is still a lot to do."

"Okay, I will see you at the carol service."

"I will see you then." Gilderoy left the cottage leaving Harmony to get on with her chores.

After the last part of the baking had been finished she stood back to admire her hard work. As it had taken the entire day to do the baking, Harmony wanted to get the kitchen clean and tidy as she wanted to get ready for the carol service before her brother got home.

Harmony gave the kitchen a thorough clean before putting the baking in the pantry, ready to cook the tea and get cleaned up before the carol service. She put the beef stew on a low heat on the stove before heading upstairs to have a bath.

While lying in the bath, her thoughts went back to her visit from Gilderoy earlier that afternoon. The thought of going to the Christmas day ball made her very nervous as she would be very much out of her comfort zone. Not wanting to burn the tea, Harmony got out of the bath before she became distracted by her thoughts.

In her room, Harmony's outfit had been picked out when she packed her clothes she would not need. As it was just a carol service at the church, she did not need to go overboard getting ready. Once her outfit had been put on she made her way downstairs to check on the simmering stew.

Even though it felt freezing outside, the aga kept the kitchen nice and warm, which warmed Harmony's father and brother when they returned from a day in the elements. Raphael entered the kitchen with his father as Harmony took the stew off the stove to see if it was cooked.

"How much longer before it is ready?" Maurice asked.

"It just needs a couple more minutes cooking time," Harmony said.

Maurice sat at the table watching his daughter then his son joined him. Harmony hated her father sitting at the table as she felt more pressure to get dinner on the table. Luckily, the next time the stew was checked it was ready. All the food was placed on the table in serving dishes so they could help themselves to whatever they wanted.

After Harmony had joined her family at the table they began their usual ritual of eating in silence. Raphael had a few questions for his sister but he knew it would be best to wait until they were out of the cottage.

When everyone had finished eating, Maurice got up from the table to go into the living room. Raphael looked at his sister. "Are you okay to do the washing-up while I get ready for the carol service?" he asked.

"Sure. It will not take me long, as I did most of it while the tea was still cooking."

Raphael left the kitchen to get ready for the carol service leaving Harmony to finish off cleaning the kitchen. As soon as she was finished in the kitchen, Harmony went up to her bedroom as she did not want to be alone in the living room with her father.

In her bedroom Harmony decided to double check everything had been packed to make sure she had not forgotten anything. No matter what, it was to be her last night in the cottage. The only thing she would truly miss would be the horses and her brother.

Harmony walked over to her window seat to look out at the fields. She looked down on the fields, picturing the horses enjoying the snow. The horses were cantering as well as whinnying to each other, while thoroughly enjoying their time in the field. As she watched, a very familiar horse decided to lie down and roll in the snow. Harmony smiled, knowing that it was Blizzard. At that moment she realised it was just a memory as Blizzard was no longer with them.

The sadness of losing Blizzard came flooding back to her as it dawned on her she would never see him play in the snow again. Harmony was looking out of her window when she heard someone stop in the doorway of her bedroom.

"What are you doing?" Raphael asked.

Harmony looked round to see her brother stood in the doorway. She turned back to look out of her window, so Raphael walked over to her.

"I am just looking out my window one last time, at the darkness," Harmony said.

Raphael sat down next to Harmony. "You know. You do not have to leave tomorrow if you do not want to."

"Father has made it very clear he does not want me here and if I do not go now I will never go. I have wanted to leave for so long, and now Father has given me the chance, I have to take it."

Raphael gave his sister a hug. "Let us get going to the carol service," he told her. He got up from the window seat then Harmony followed.

CHAPTER THIRTY

The two of them put their shoes on before leaving the cottage.

"You go and get Pandora while I get her harness," Raphael instructed.

Harmony walked over to the stables while her brother went to the tack room. She walked into the stable to take the horse's rug off. Just as she hung the rug over the stable door her brother arrived with Pandora's harness.

"Can you put this on her while I get the cart ready?" Raphael asked.

"Sure." Harmony took the harness from her brother before turning back to the horse. "I guess he wants us to get going," Harmony told Pandora while she placed the harness on her back.

Once the horse was in her harness, Harmony walked her over to the cart where she helped her brother hitch Pandora up to the cart. They climbed aboard the cart ready to set off for the church in Elvesbridge.

"Are you looking forward to the carol service?" Raphael asked.

"Yes I am. I like singing Christmas carols as it adds to the magic and tradition of this time of year," Harmony said.

Raphael decided to ask the questions he had wanted to ask his sister once they were alone. "Have you sorted out where you are going to go when you leave tomorrow?"

"Yes, a friend is helping me out."

"So, you are going back to the humans then?"

"No."

"What?" Raphael asked perplexed.

"I am staying with the elves," Harmony said, amused by the expression on her brother's face.

"Who are you going to be staying with?" Raphael asked.

"I will be staying with the servants at Elveshire castle."

"You will be working for Pixel's family?"

"Only as a patrol rider, I will be with the horses all day."

As they approached the church they spotted lots of people walking in. Harmony became more nervous as they got closer as it was her first carol service with the elves.

"Are you okay?" Raphael asked.

"Just nervous, as this is kind of new to me."

"What are you nervous about?"

"I do not want to embarrass myself in front of everyone."

"You will not embarrass yourself," Raphael told her.

"How do you know?" Harmony asked.

"I just do." Raphael stopped Pandora alongside the other horses and carriages.

They both climbed out of the cart surprised to see so many elves. Harmony spotted a few of the patrol riders with their families. Trixie waved at her friend as she passed by with her family.

Raphael led the way over to the church following the crowd. As they got nearer to the church, Raphael spotted Amos. Rhoda was stood just behind him talking to somebody. As Harmony got closer to them she realised Rhoda was talking to Pixel. Pixel smiled when he saw Harmony approaching.

"What are you doing here?" Harmony asked before greeting him properly.

"I meant what I said when your father decided to throw you out. I am going to stick by you no matter what," Pixel said.

The five of them followed the rest of the parishioners into the church. They all managed to sit together on one of the pews. Amos sat closest to the wall then Rhoda followed by Raphael then Harmony and Pixel sat on the end.

Each of them had been given a booklet which told them the order in which things were going to happen during the carol service. While Harmony sat waiting for the last people to enter the church, she flicked through to see which carols they would be singing.

The service started with everyone singing *The Holly And The Ivy*. After the first carol there were a couple of readings before everyone stood up to sing *O Come All Ye Faithful*. There were a couple more readings which Harmony used as an opportunity to look around the church at the architecture. The congregation rose to their feet for the penultimate carol of *Hark The Herald Angels Sing*. Everyone took a seat for the vicar to do the last reading. For the final carol they sang *Once In Royal David's City*.

Everybody remained standing while the royal family exited the church before following them out. Harmony, Raphael, Amos, Rhoda and Pixel were stood outside the church talking.

"Pixel, why do you not come back to ours for Christmas?" Raphael asked.

"That would be lovely," Pixel replied.

They each wished each other a merry Christmas before going their separate ways. On their way back to Pandora, Pixel grabbed Shadow. Harmony and Raphael climbed in the cart while Pixel mounted on to Shadow.

As they went to leave Pixel had a thought. "I do not have any nightwear or spare clothes with me."

"You can borrow mine," Raphael offered.

On the way home it began to snow. Harmony spent most of the journey watching the snow fall. Pixel was riding next to the cart so he could watch her. Raphael kept his eyes on the road as it was busy with everyone heading home. By the time they got back to the cottage the snow began to settle.

"It looks like we are going to have a white Christmas," Raphael stated, breaking the silence.

CHAPTER THIRTY-ONE

When they arrived at the stable-yard Pixel dismounted from Shadow while Harmony and Raphael climbed out of the cart.

"You two go into the cottage and I will see to the horses," Raphael told them.

Starting to feel the cold, Harmony and Pixel made their way to the cottage. The two of them entered through the back door, feeling the warmth starting to defrost them. Not wanting to see her father, Harmony led Pixel straight upstairs.

As Pixel entered Harmony's bedroom, he was surprised to see that pretty much all her stuff had been packed into bags. Harmony had sat on her bed waiting for Pixel to comment on how empty her bedroom was.

"Not long now," Pixel reminded her.

"I know, I cannot wait," Harmony said excitedly.

Pixel walked over to Harmony's bed. He sat beside her and took hold of her hand. Harmony looked up at Pixel. They stared into each other's eyes. Harmony leaned forward causing Pixel to do the same. Before they knew it, the two of them were kissing. They quickly broke apart when they heard someone coming up the stairs. Raphael stopped in the doorway of his sister's bedroom. "Here are some night clothes for Pixel," Raphael said handing the clothes to Pixel.

"Thank you," Pixel said as he took the clothes from Raphael.

"Goodnight, you two," Raphael said trying not to smile as he left the room.

"Goodnight," Harmony and Pixel replied.

Pixel looked at Harmony. "Where am I supposed to sleep?"

"Well, you have two options. There is the spare bedroom, or you could stay in here."

Pixel had to think about it, as elves did not usually share a room with women unless they were married. After a little bit of thought Pixel decided to take a leaf out of Gilderoy's book. "It will mean breaking the rules, but I think I will stay in here," he told her.

"A rebel, I like it," Harmony told him. She seemed pleased that he had chosen to stay in her room.

Harmony walked across the landing to get the bedding from the spare bedroom. When she returned to her room, Pixel was lying on her bed. She walked over to the window to look at the snow. Pixel blew out the candle then went to stand behind her. He wrapped his arms around Harmony's waist causing her to lean back against him.

"It looks so magical," Harmony told him.

"It is even more magical looking at it with you," Pixel told her. He let go of Harmony before walking back over to her bed. He lay down then patted the space beside him.

Harmony picked up her nightgown before making her way to the bathroom to get changed into her nightwear. Whilst in the bathroom she thought about whether she was doing the right thing. Harmony still loved Damien, but did Damien still love her after what had happened at the try-outs?

Harmony got changed then went back to her room. She threw her dress on the floor before climbing into bed next to Pixel. She looked across at Pixel noticing that while she had been in the bathroom he took the opportunity to change his clothes before getting under the covers. He threw the covers over Harmony before the two of them snuggled under the duvet, settling down for the night.

CHAPTER THIRTY-TWO

The next morning when Harmony woke up her room seemed bright. It was not the sunlight making it brighter, the only thing it could be was snow.

Harmony got out of bed to go to her window. As soon as she got out the covers she felt how cold the air had turned. Harmony grabbed her dressing gown off the end of her bed throwing it on quickly.

Harmony slowly walked over to her window. As she opened the curtains she found everything covered in snow. To Harmony it was exactly how Christmas should be. She stood enjoying the crisp white scenery in front of her when there was movement behind her. Harmony turned just as Pixel sat up in bed.

"Merry Christmas," Harmony said cheerfully.

"Merry Christmas," Pixel replied, half asleep. He thought it was too early for someone to be so jolly.

Harmony sat on the bed next to Pixel.

"When shall we head downstairs?" Pixel asked.

"After we have got dressed," Harmony said as she got up from the bed.

Harmony picked up the red dress she had set aside for that day and made her way to the bathroom to get ready. The whole time Harmony was getting ready she thought about how much she liked having Pixel around.

Having got washed and dressed, Harmony went back to her room to do her hair. She sat down on the stool at her dressing table. As she looked in the mirror she noticed Pixel had got dressed while she had been in the bathroom. Harmony decided to do a couple of small plaits next to her face before pinning them back with a couple of sparkly clips.

"You look beautiful," Pixel complimented her.

"Thank you," Harmony replied. She led the way out of her bedroom down to the living room.

When Harmony looked in the living room she noticed piles of presents next to the chairs and sofa. Maurice had already taken his place in his chair. Raphael sat in the other wingback chair leaving the sofa for Harmony and Pixel. They all said merry Christmas to each other before opening their piles of presents.

Harmony's first present was from Raphael. She took the paper off to discover a little rectangular box. She lifted the lid to find a charm bracelet with different horses on it. Harmony thanked her brother before moving on to her next present.

The next present Harmony picked up she read the label to find the present was from an anonymous person. Curious as to who it could be from, Harmony quickly tore off the paper. Inside was another little box. She opened the lid of the box to find a heart-shaped locket. Also inside the box Harmony spotted a note. Trying not to attract attention to herself she quietly opened the piece of paper. The note read:

To my darling Harmony,

Now you truly own my heart which will belong to you forever. Even when we are apart you just have to open the locket to remember me. If we never get to be together you will always be my one true love.

I miss you loads, thinking of you every minute of every day.

Love you always
Damien xxx

When Harmony looked up from the note she saw the other three looking at her. It was only then that she realised she had tears in her eyes. The others were looking at her, puzzled by how emotional she had become over the present.

"Who was the present from?" Raphael asked.

Harmony looked at her father before looking at Raphael. "The present was from Damien."

Everyone looked at Maurice, to find his expression had changed from puzzled to angry. Knowing that her father had become angry, Harmony decided to go to her room while he calmed down. Maurice went out to the kitchen to make a start on the Christmas dinner.

Raphael and Pixel looked at each other, both unsure of what to do. Neither of them were sure if Harmony wanted to be alone or not. Guessing that she would probably be thinking about Damien, they decided it would be best to leave her alone. The two of them sat in silence wishing they had something to do.

Not long after leaving the living room, Harmony cautiously walked down the stairs to make sure her father had not returned to the living room. When Raphael saw his sister he thought it might be a good idea to think of an activity outside the cottage for a little while. "How about we take the horses their Christmas presents?" he asked.

"I would like to see Tyson," Harmony said. Not wanting to go through the kitchen, she led the way out the front door round the side of the cottage before going through the back garden.

When the three of them got to the stables, Harmony walked straight over to Tyson. She gave him a hug before heading over to the feed room. As it was cold, the horses were given their breakfast in their stables.

Harmony prepared each of their feeds before cutting up the apples and carrots she had got the horses for Christmas. After adding the apples and carrots to the feeds she carried a couple of feed buckets out to the stables.

While Harmony had been preparing the feed, the boys had been dealing with the water buckets. Harmony put Tyson's feed in his stable before taking Spring his feed. She went back to the feed room to grab a couple more feed buckets. As she walked in, Raphael had picked up a couple of buckets as well. Harmony did not mind as it meant getting back to the warm cottage quicker.

After sorting the horses out the three of them decided to go back to the cottage to warm up. On the way back to the cottage they listened to the snow crunching underfoot.

Raphael knew that his sister would rather have stayed outside than going back to where her father would be. Surprisingly, Harmony did not mind going back to the cottage as much as she thought she would. Knowing Pixel was with her she felt she could stand up to her father, it also helped that she had Damien's locket hanging around her neck.

Raphael was just about to go back round the front of the cottage to avoid their father when Harmony opened the back door. Knowing his sister knew what she was doing he decided to follow. Harmony walked through the kitchen and into the living room.

When they entered the living room they were pleased to see that the wood burning stove had already been lit. As the three of them sat warming up, the pleasant smell of the dinner started to enter the room.

"Nothing better than the smell of a Christmas dinner cooking to make you feel festive," Harmony commented.

Raphael started opening the rest of his presents then Harmony realised she had more presents as well. Whilst waiting for the dinner to cook, they each took to doing different activities. Raphael had started reading a book he had been given that morning. Pixel had gone upstairs to talk to his family on his phone about the ball. Harmony had taken to looking at the locket Damien had given her. She also took another look at the note that came with it.

Pixel got to the bottom of the stairs as Maurice announced that lunch was ready. Raphael led the way to the kitchen followed by Pixel and Harmony.

As everyone walked into the kitchen they were surprised to find the table had a red and gold tablecloth on it. It had festive placemats and coasters too.

Harmony took her seat, eager to get lunch over with. Raphael could tell Harmony had something planned for the afternoon. It worried him because there was only one thing he knew she wanted to do.

Maurice put the plates on the table then reminded everyone to pull their crackers first. Pixel pulled his cracker with Harmony while Raphael pulled his cracker with his father. After all the crackers had been pulled everyone put their Christmas hats on.

Harmony kept looking at her father wishing things could have been different between them. Once all the food had been eaten Raphael asked his sister what she had planned for the afternoon. She told him she planned to visit their mother's grave. Maurice looked at his daughter, unsure of her plans. Raphael knew as soon as his sister left the cottage she would not come back.

Harmony left the table, so Pixel got up and followed. The two of them went up to Harmony's bedroom. When they got to her bedroom Pixel asked her what she was really planning to do. She turned to look at Pixel. "It is time for me to leave," she told him.

Pixel had a feeling that Harmony was just using going to her mother's grave as an excuse to get away. "Where is your car?" he asked.

"It is out the front," Harmony said. She picked up a couple of the bags so Pixel grabbed a couple as well.

The two of them quietly made their way downstairs to the hall. Pixel told Harmony to bring down the rest of the bags as fast as she could. Not wanting to leave without saying goodbye to her brother she poked her head around the doorframe. Raphael was stood in the kitchen alone. He walked over to his sister. "You are not leaving, are you?" he asked.

"I have to. I cannot stay trapped any longer," Harmony said, and they held each other in a warm embrace.

Pixel walked into the kitchen. "After we have gone I need you to get Tyson ready for travelling. I am going to send one of the stable-hands to fetch him, so keep your father in the cottage," he instructed.

Raphael nodded as they heard Maurice on his way back to the cottage. Pixel and Harmony quickly grabbed Harmony's things making a quick getaway. Once they were out of the cottage the two of them relaxed.

"Where do you want to go?" Pixel asked.

"I am going to drive to the cemetery to visit my mother's grave."

Pixel climbed in the passenger side of the car as Harmony climbed in the driver's side. Harmony started the car then began the journey to the cemetery. She concentrated on driving, trying not to think too much about where they were heading. As they approached the cemetery Harmony became tense.

"Are you sure you want to do this?" Pixel asked.

"I am certain," Harmony said.

After she had parked the car, Pixel got out. Harmony paused for a moment before joining him.

Pixel led the way into the graveyard. He could feel Harmony's hand getting tighter around his the closer they got to her mother's grave. Sooner than she expected, Pixel stopped. Harmony looked up to see why he had stopped.

"Here it is," Pixel informed her.

As Harmony started to read the words on her mother's headstone, it wasn't long before she began to weep. Pixel wrapped his arm around her shoulders pulling her into a side hug.

Guessing that she was not likely to calm down until they left, he guided her out of the cemetery. As they approached the car, Harmony looked up at Pixel. He could see she wanted to apologise for her reaction. He gave her one last reassuring hug before taking the car keys from her.

This time Pixel drove with Harmony sat in the passenger seat. Harmony was slowly calming down the further they got from the cemetery.

"Where are we going?" she asked.

"We are going back to my castle," Pixel replied.

Harmony looked out the window at the unfamiliar scenery. A couple of times Pixel noticed her looking at the locket Damien had bought her. "Are you sure you want to come and live at my castle?" he asked.

"Of course I do. I am actually looking forward to it."

"When we get to the castle I will introduce you to my family, and then we can open our presents."

"I did not buy any presents for your family," Harmony told him.

"I already took care of that." Pixel smiled.

"When will the ball be?" she asked.

"It will be later in the evening."

Harmony looked out the window admiring the approach to Elveshire Castle. She looked at the oak trees lining either side of the driveway with fields beyond. In each of the fields were herds of fallow deer.

When the stone castle came into view, Harmony loved how it looked like the kind of castle children built out of sand on the beach. A square castle with a turret at each of the four corners. Surrounding the front of the castle stood a stone balcony with steps leading up to the front door.

CHAPTER THIRTY-THREE

When they arrived at the castle some of the servants were stood outside waiting for them. Pixel got out of the car followed by Harmony. He turned to each of the servants giving them jobs to do. He asked the stable-hand to fetch Tyson from the cottage. The two maids he instructed to take Harmony's belongings up to a bedroom in the servants' quarters. Just as the maids were about to start unloading the car, one of the footmen came out to help them.

Once everything had been emptied out of the car Harmony and Pixel took the car down to the stables to be parked with the horseboxes out of sight.

The two of them walked back to the castle in comfortable silence, allowing Harmony to take in her new surroundings. The last time Harmony had been at the castle she had had too much on her mind to notice anything around her. She was also feeling nervous about meeting Pixel's family formally for the first time. She was listening closely to the sound of the snow crunching under their feet, hoping it would calm her nerves. Before Harmony knew it, they were stood outside the front door of the castle. Pixel looked at Harmony who was staring at the solid front door in front of her.

"You will be fine," Pixel reassured her.

Harmony looked at the door before taking a deep breath then slowly releasing it.

"Are you ready?" Pixel asked.

Once again Harmony nodded as she could not speak. The front door opened, allowing them to enter. When Harmony looked at who had opened the door it was the footman who had helped the maids unload her car.

As Harmony entered the grand entrance hall she was met with the sight of a sweeping staircase that led to the rooms on the first floor. After admiring the brightly-coloured entrance hall, Pixel led Harmony to a room to which the door was already open.

Inside the living room Harmony noticed the cold tiled floor had changed to a soft warm carpet as they entered the bright, airy new room. In front of her, the tall windows not only let in lots of light, they perfectly framed the snow-covered grounds outside. Harmony then looked around the room, admiring the rest of it.

Pixel's family were gathered on three sofas that were surrounding an open fireplace. In front of the fire lying on a rug were a pair of smooth collies. In the corner of the room stood a tall Christmas tree surrounded by presents.

Harmony walked with Pixel over to the sofas. As she walked further into the room the warmth coming from the open fire hit her. They were almost at the sofas when Harmony decided to watch the dogs who were sprawled out enjoying the heat from the fire. Seeing the dogs made her smile as she had always loved dogs.

When Harmony joined Pixel's family he introduced her to everyone.

"Please take a seat," queen Clementina offered.

Harmony sat on one of the sofas next to Gilderoy and Pixel.

"Can we start opening presents now?" Gilderoy asked.

"Yes, you may," Clementina replied.

Two footmen entered the room to begin handing out the presents. He handed everyone a present including Harmony. Pixel watched her out of the corner of his eye as did Gilderoy.

Harmony unwrapped the first present to reveal a shoebox. She lifted the lid to reveal a sparkly pair of strappy sandals. Harmony could not believe how beautiful they were or how expensive they looked.

"Thank you, Goliath, they are beautiful," Harmony said, holding up one of the shoes admiring it. She placed the shoes in the box on the floor.

The next present she opened contained a jewellery set from Gilderoy. Harmony thanked him before moving on to her next present. The rest of her presents contained, a shawl, a tiara, a pair of elbow-length silver gloves, as well as a stunning light-blue princess-style ball gown that had sparkly detailing throughout the corset-style bodice and skirt.

"Thank you so much, everyone. The gifts are amazing," Harmony told them.

"Pixel, where is your present for Harmony?" Clementina asked.

"I am going to give it to her now. If everybody could please follow me," Pixel replied.

They all got up from the sofas to follow Pixel. He led them through the entrance hall to the front door.

"Why are we going outside?" Marko asked.

"You will see," Pixel replied.

As they walked through the front door they saw one of the stable-hands holding a light brown and white horse.

"What do you think?" Pixel asked.

"He is absolutely gorgeous," Harmony said.

"I am glad you like your Christmas present," Pixel said.

"What?" Harmony asked turning to look at Pixel.

"He is your new horse. I knew you did not have a horse for patrol rider duties therefore I decided to buy you one."

Harmony was smiling, feeling happy that the amazing looking horse in front of her belonged to her. "Thank you so much. I absolutely love him," she said and made her way down the steps to the horse then began stroking him.

"What are you going to call him?" Gilderoy asked.

"I think I will call him Jolly Jester," she said and went back to admiring her new horse.

"Okay, everyone, we have got a couple of hours before we need to start getting ready for the ball. During that time, I would like to see all the Christmas presents taken to your bedrooms," king Nelson instructed.

"Where will Harmony be getting ready?" Pixel asked.

"I have put her in the lavender room for tonight," Clementina replied.

"I think we should use some of the time teaching Harmony some of the formalities for the ball," Goliath told them.

"You boys had better get started," Nelson instructed. He left the boys outside while he entered the castle with Clementina.

Harmony started heading up the steps to the castle to do what Pixel's parents had instructed them to do.

"Where are you going?" Pixel asked.

"To move my presents like your parents asked us to," Harmony replied.

The boys followed Harmony into the castle then the stable hand walked Jolly Jester back to the stables.

Inside the castle everyone was in the living room picking up their presents to take them up to their rooms. Harmony struggled to carry all her boxes as well as her long dress, so both Pixel and Goliath helped her.

CHAPTER THIRTY-FOUR

After clearing all the presents from the living room, Pixel and his brothers began preparing Harmony for the ball.

They explained that all the guests would be gathered in the entrance hall waiting for them to enter down the stairs. Goliath informed her that Marko and Stefan would enter first followed by Pixel, '...and you then I will enter with Gilderoy leaving our parents until last."

All the boys walked to the top of the stairs with Harmony before turning to face the bottom.

"What are we doing?" Harmony asked.

"Practising, I thought it would be good for you to run through it a couple of times," Pixel said.

The princes got into position so Harmony took her place next to Pixel. He took hold of her arm to get her used to walking down the stairs in a formal manner.

"When do you greet each of the guests?" Harmony asked.

"After we have entered the ballroom," Pixel said.

"Will there be anyone I know at the ball?" she asked.

"The patrol riders will be there with their families. The protectors will be around and Freedom will be there with her family," Goliath said.

"You have got to be kidding me," Harmony said.

"Just ignore Freedom, she will probably be annoyed anyway," Pixel told her.

"Why would Freedom be annoyed?" Harmony asked.

"You are here as Pixel's guest and Freedom does not like it if she is not the most important person around," Marko replied.

The boys had been teaching Harmony the basic etiquette for so long that by the time they were done it was time for Harmony to begin getting ready.

Clementina showed Harmony to the bedroom she would be staying in. When the two of them reached the room, they entered to find the head housemaid stood waiting for them. The housemaid curtseyed, so Clementina began introductions. She first introduced the head housemaid to Harmony as a young lady named Clara. She then introduced Harmony to Clara.

Once all the introductions were done, Clementina made her way over to the door. "I shall leave you in the capable hands of Clara and I will see you later for the ball," she told Harmony.

Harmony nodded, so Clementina left the room.

"Your bath is ready for you, miss," Clara informed her.

Harmony followed Clara in to the en-suite bathroom that had been decorated in the finest white marble. In the middle of the room stood a free-standing roll-top bath filled with bubbles.

"I will lay your undergarments out in the dressing room for when you are finished," Clara informed her.

"Thank you," Harmony said before making her way over to the bath. She waited until Clara left the room before undressing and getting into the water. While she was relaxing, Harmony realised the next dress she would be putting on would be the big ball gown she had been given for Christmas. Harmony was enjoying the warmth of the bath when there was a knock on the door.

"Who is it?" Harmony asked.

"It is Clara, miss."

"Come in."

Clara opened the door and entered. "I have come to wash your hair."

Harmony sat up to allow Clara to wash her hair. She found it strange to have somebody wash her hair for her, and when Clara had finished, she used a towel to dry it off a bit. "When you have put your corset on let me know and I will come and tighten it for you," Clara instructed.

Harmony nodded, so Clara left the bathroom allowing Harmony to get out of the bath. She dried herself before making her way into the dressing room. Laid out on a bench in front of her were a pair of bloomers and a corset. Before putting the garments on, she grabbed some underwear from her bag that had been put in the dressing room. She climbed into the underwear as well as the other undergarments before making her way into the bedroom where Clara was stood next to the bed waiting for her.

"If you come over to the bed I will tighten the corset for you," Clara told her.

Harmony walked over to the bed unsure of having the corset tightened as it felt tight enough.

"Hold on to the bed so I do not pull you over," Clara instructed.

Harmony leaned against the bedpost while Clara began pulling on the lace of the corset, tightening it. She was not used to wearing a corset which felt restrictive. After Clara had finished the corset, Harmony moved away from the bed.

"How does it feel?" Clara asked.

"Very weird," Harmony said.

"You will get used to it the longer you wear it."

"What is next?" Harmony asked.

"Your hair and makeup." Clara helped Harmony into a dressing gown before leading her over to the dressing table and sitting her down on the stool.

"Are you doing my hair and makeup?" Harmony asked.

"No, miss. Clementina has got a hairdresser and makeup artist for you."

The room was silent, then there was a knock on the door. Clara walked over to the door to answer it. "Come in."

Harmony looked round to see a woman enter with a bag on her shoulder as well as one in her hand.

"Good evening, Harmony. Shall we get started?" the woman asked.

"Okay," Harmony replied smiling. She turned to face the mirror making it easier for the lady to start on her hair. "What style are you going to do my hair?"

"It will be something that suits you, following the guidelines Clementina gave me," the lady replied.

Harmony sat looking in the mirror while the hairdresser started playing with her hair. Now that she had started getting ready for the ball she could feel the nerves building as she was going to be dressed up in front of people she did not know. Harmony sat thinking about the ball when someone knocked on the door.

Clara made her way across the room and opened the door. Stood at the door was one of the footman holding a cube-shaped box. "Could you give this to Harmony, it is from Prince Pixel?"

"Of course," Clara replied. She took the box from the footman and closed the door. She placed the box with the other accessory boxes. After placing the box down she started carrying some of the accessories over to the dressing table.

Clara lifted the lid off the tiara box allowing the hairdresser to carefully pick it up, placing it on Harmony's head before securing it in place. Next Clara took over the jewellery for the hairdresser to put in place after she had finished the makeup.

Once the hairdresser had finished, Harmony looked in the mirror surprised by how different she looked with makeup on and her hair done. She thanked the hairdresser before she left, leaving Harmony alone once again with Clara.

Clara walked over to the dress bag that had been placed on the bed. "Okay, Harmony, time to put your dress on," she informed her.

Suddenly, Harmony was hit by a wave of nerves. She could not remember a time that she had felt so nervous. She slowly got up before making her way over to Clara. She removed the dressing gown then Clara removed the dress from the bag, lowering it to the floor allowing Harmony to step into it. After pulling the dress up, Clara began lacing up the back while Harmony held the dress in place.

"Go and sit back down on the stool. I will finish putting the rest of the accessories on," Clara instructed.

Harmony made her way over to the stool, moving for the first time in her dress. She sat down carefully making sure her dress was flat.

"What did Prince Pixel get you?" Clara asked.

Harmony lifted the lid of the box to reveal a blue, white and silver rose corsage. She slid it on her wrist smiling at the colour scheme Pixel's family had chosen for her. Harmony held out her arm showing Clara the corsage Pixel had given her.

As soon as Clara felt sure everything was in place she took Harmony over to the full-length mirror to see what she looked like. "What do you think?" Clara asked.

"I cannot believe that is me. It looks amazing. Now it all seems real, yet I cannot believe it is. I would never have dreamed that I would be going to a royal ball in a castle on Christmas Day with a prince."

Clara walked towards the bedroom door. "I do believe your prince is waiting in the corridor for you with his brothers," she informed her.

Harmony turned to face Clara. She stood for a moment, the nerves finally reaching their peak as she realised she would be leaving the room to go to a ball with a prince. When Harmony started smiling at Clara the maid opened the bedroom door.

CHAPTER THIRTY-FIVE

In the corridor the princes turned around when they heard the door behind them open. The boys stood waiting for Harmony to come out so they could see what she looked like. When Harmony emerged from the bedroom the boys could not believe their eyes.

Pixel walked over to Harmony. "You look breathtakingly beautiful," he said.

"Thank you. I like how the colours of your outfit match mine," Harmony said happily.

"It is time for us to go to the ball," Goliath informed them.

They all got in order, ready to make their way down the stairs like they had practised. As they got closer to the stairs the voices of the guests grew louder. Harmony tried her hardest to block out the voices, but they were just too loud. She knew if her arm had not been touching Pixel's she would probably be panicking.

"Are you okay?" Pixel asked.

"Not exactly."

"Just remember what we rehearsed."

"Which was what?"

"You will be fine."

Marko and Stefan walked down the stairs first, followed by Gilderoy and Goliath. At that moment Harmony realised the guests were commenting on whoever walked down the stairs. It concerned her, what would they say about her. An elf raised by humans, now on the arm of an elvish prince. She slowly walked down the stairs making sure she kept the correct posture as she walked.

When they reached the bottom of the stairs, Pixel and Harmony went and stood in front of the guests facing the staircase. Now they were in place it was time for Clementina and Nelson to enter.

Everybody fell silent as they looked towards the stairs. Clementina and Nelson entered just as Harmony and Pixel had done. Everyone watched in awe as they came down the stairs together. As Harmony watched Clementina, she hoped she had been as elegant and graceful as she came down the stairs.

Once the two of them reached the bottom of the stairs they walked past the guests who all bowed or curtseyed. The princes were bowing too, so as Clementina and Nelson approached, Harmony curtseyed just like she had been taught in her dance classes.

When Harmony stood back up she could see Pixel smiling at her. She knew no one would have expected her to know any of the etiquette in a situation like that but through her dancing as well as a general interest she knew a lot.

After the grand entrance of the royal family, the butler entered the room to make an announcement. "Dinner is served," he informed everyone.

The guests cleared a pathway to the ballroom, making way for the king and queen to enter the room first followed by their sons. As they entered the room they were greeted by round tables covered by burgundy tablecloths and gold table runners. On each of the tables stood five-arm gold candelabras that had ivory candles in them, that had been lit to provide a soft tranquil light to the room.

Harmony walked with Pixel and his family over to a stone platform which had a rectangular table that had been decorated with the same décor as the round tables.

Everyone stood behind their chairs, waiting for the king and queen to take their seats then the guests could be seated. Once everyone had taken their seats, the servants began serving the starters. The room fell silent of conversation, making the sound of cutlery on chinaware the only sound to be heard throughout the room. When everyone had finished eating, conversation struck up once again.

Freedom was looking up at the head table watching Harmony talk to a couple of the princes. "How come she gets to sit up there?" she asked her mother in a whiney voice.

Her mother looked round at her daughter. "She is the guest of one of the princes, hence she gets to sit with them," she said, annoyed at her daughter's behaviour. She felt pleased to see that the servants were now bringing the main course which was a traditional Christmas dinner.

Once again the room became silent but this time Harmony could feel someone staring at her. She looked around the room until she spotted Freedom looking at her. Not wanting to let Freedom get to her she looked away returning to her dinner.

"Are you okay?" Pixel asked.

"I am fine, just Freedom trying to get to me with her mind games."

After the dessert of Christmas pudding had been eaten, the guests departed from the ballroom to allow the servants to clear the room ready for the ball. The ladies retired to the living room while the men retired to the library.

In the living room Harmony was trying her best to stay away from Freedom. When it seemed impossible to avoid her, Clementina called her over to talk to a lady Harmony had never seen before. Even though she did not know the lady, she felt glad to be out of reach of Freedom.

After socialising for a while, the guests returned to the ballroom ready for the ball to begin. Once all the guests had entered the ballroom the doors were closed behind them. Everyone turned to face the doors, awaiting the arrival of the royal family.

The king and queen entered through the doors making their way to the middle of the room. Once they were in position the orchestra began playing a classic waltz. After they had taken a turn around the dance floor it was time for the princes to join in with their partners.

Freedom watched on, full of hope that Pixel would choose her as his dance partner just like he had done every year. Her confidence grew as he started heading in her direction. Freedom's confidence suddenly turned to disappointment when he made his way over to Harmony who was stood a few people away. She watched as each of the princes picked a patrol rider to be their dance partners, leaving Freedom stood with her parents.

Pixel walked with Harmony to the dance floor before turning her to face him. "Do you know this dance?" he asked.

"I think I can remember it. It has been years since I last danced a waltz."

"Just go with the flow of the dance," Pixel told her.

The two of them began dancing the waltz around the dance floor. Harmony let Pixel lead while she tried her best to remember all the steps. Pixel smiled at Harmony, hoping she would now relax and start having fun.

The waltz ended so Pixel and Harmony separated. When the orchestra began playing again Pixel leaned towards Harmony. "Would you like to dance the foxtrot with me?"

"I would love to."

The two of them came together once again then began dancing the foxtrot around the dance floor. This time when Pixel smiled at her she smiled back. Pixel felt pleased to see Harmony finally enjoying herself. Once the foxtrot had ended, Harmony walked away from the dance floor, so Pixel followed.

"Harmony, are you okay?" Pixel asked.

"I am fine, I just need some fresh air," she replied, and made her way out on to the balcony to have a few moments alone. As she rested on the stone balustrade she heard someone behind her.

"What are you doing here, Harmony?" Freedom asked from the doorway of the castle.

"I used to ask myself the exact same question. Now that I have a job, I have friends and I have family, I have a reason to be here," Harmony said.

"You may have all those things, but Pixel is mine. You may have embarrassed me this evening by taking him away from me in front of everyone, but I promise you, I will never let it happen again."

Harmony turned to face her ex best friend. "I did not take Pixel away from you; he chose me to be his guest to the ball."

Freedom made her way out on to the balcony to stand behind Harmony who had once again turned her back to her.

"Face it, Harmony, you do not belong here."

"You are right, and I cannot argue with that. Fact is, I do not belong anywhere," Harmony told her.

The two of them were stood in silence when they heard footsteps approaching from behind. When the person reached the entranceway, the footsteps stopped.

"Freedom, time you went back inside, your parents are looking for you," Pixel informed her.

Freedom turned away from Harmony to make her way back into the castle. When she reached Pixel, she stopped, grabbing hold of his arm.

"Let go of my arm," Pixel instructed.

"Come and dance with me," she ordered pulling on his arm.

"No. Now let go."

"Please come and dance with me," Freedom begged desperately.

Pixel tried to pull his arm from Freedom's grasp but ended up pulling her closer. "Freedom, just because Goliath would not dance with you, do not think for one moment that I or any of my brothers would for that matter," he told her sternly.

Freedom let go of his arm. "Fine, go be with the human lover, see if I care," she told him.

Pixel made his way out on to the balcony with Harmony, leaving Freedom stood in the doorway. As she turned to walk across the entrance hall she spotted the princes stood looking at her a few feet away. After hearing what Freedom had said they made their way towards the door.

"Where are you all going?" Freedom asked.

"We are going to be with the human lover. We would choose her over you any day," Gilderoy replied.

The boys walked out to the front balcony where Harmony stood leaning against the stone balustrade looking up at the sky. Pixel looked at Gilderoy when his brothers approached them. "You do realise that she will inform Mother of what you said to her."

"I do not care. Freedom had no right talking about Harmony like that," Gilderoy told his brother.

The brothers made their way over to Harmony, who seemed fascinated by the pitch black abyss above.

"So, Harmony, what do you make of all this?" Goliath asked.

"Right now, it feels strange but I am enjoying it."

"Does that mean you have made your decision?" Pixel asked.

"I believe I have," Harmony answered as she turned to face them.

"What is your decision?" Gilderoy asked.

"I am going to stay with the elves," she said.

All the boys cheered then hugged Harmony, pleased with her decision.

"Now we just need to find your happily ever after," Gilderoy told her.

Harmony looked at Goliath then smiled before turning her attention back to Gilderoy. "I think I already know just what my happily ever after would be," Harmony told them.

"What is it?" Marko asked curious to know.

"I think I know," Goliath replied.

"Tell me," Marko pleaded.

"You will just have to wait and see," Harmony told him.

Harmony and Pixel smiled at each other before she returned to looking at the stars again. As she watched the stars shine brightly she wondered if she would get her happily ever after.

The End

Lightning Source UK Ltd.
Milton Keynes UK
UKHW012221070920
369495UK00004B/1255